Excerpts from an Unknown Guidebook

Book I: Phases of the Moon

by Josef Bastian
Illustrations by Patrick McEvoy

"Excerpts from an Unknown Guidebook,
Book 1: Phases of the Moon"

Copyright © 2018 Josef Bastian
All rights reserved

No part of this publication may be reproduced, distributed, or transmitted in any form or by any means, including photocopying, recording, digital scanning, or other electronic or mechanical methods, without the prior written permission of the publisher, except in the case of brief quotations embodied in critical reviews and certain other noncommercial uses permitted by copyright law.

For permission requests, please address

Folkteller
407 Webster
Royal Oak, MI 48073

Published 2018 by Folkteller
Printed in the United States of America

20 19 18   1 2 3 4

HC: 978-1-7320890-0-6
PB: 978-1-7320890-1-3
eBook: 978-1-7320890-2-0

Library of Congress Control Number: 2018936429

Acknowledgements

For my family, friends, and our first Tellerians:

Megan Dusablon

Brady Longmuir

Danny Weickel

Anthony Martinez

Lacey Martinez

Justin DeHaai

Anna Laube

Demetrius Urban

Dominic Urban

Zander Carroll

Megan Schafer

Ryan Schafer

Anthony Vecellio

Your hearts know in silence the secrets
of the days and the nights.

But your ears thirst for the sound
of your heart's knowledge.

—Kahlil Gibran

Stories that dare not be read must be told.

—From the Folkteller's Guidebook

Incipit

(So, it begins)

Prologue

Now I agree, it may seem odd or even a bit self-absorbed for a Folkteller like me to be telling you stories about folktelling. However, if you think that this is just an exercise in ego, selfish oratory, and grand gesturing, I must protest. I ply my craft of storytelling as my predecessors have for millennia. I am no braggart, though I do pride myself in spinning tales of wonder and enchantment that will compel you to listen and read on.

So, I beg of you dear readers and listeners, to join me as I share a story that speaks a little of the origins and struggles of my people.

It's true, we are a mysterious and secretive breed who are often forced to operate in the shadows, though we are bearers of light. We are the ones who share the stories that need to be heard with the people that need to hear them. And sometimes people don't want to hear what we have to say. In such cases, things can get very interesting. For though we bear the message, we have no control of what will happen once the message is received.

That's the odd thing about folktelling. I always know how things will begin, but I never know how they will end.

So, with that said, let's just begin…

The following note was scrawled by a fugitive Folkteller. Pages from his secret book have been scattered across various parts of the world. This section was discovered in a small-town library in the Midwest near an odd stack of loose papers. The story you are about to read was drawn from these mysterious writings.

To Whom It May Concern,

You don't know me, and I don't know you. That's a good thing. I'll keep the stories coming for as long as I can.

They must never find out that I'm doing this, that I'm opening up these pages to you. If I'm caught, it will mean my death.

They think I'm a traitor, but I'm not. I have to do this. It's the only way to save us—all of us.

Read the stories, tell the others, and share what you've learned—before it's too late.

I will write again when I can.

Yours in Faith and Confidence,
X

1
The Empty House

Every great adventure begins between the arms of an ordinary day. This adventure is no different.

Aaron was a sandy-haired, slightly built teen from a quite unremarkable background. In fact, you might say that he suffered from *Middleitis*.

This was a non-medical condition from which many eighth graders suffered. Symptoms of this teenage malady included being invisible to girls, feeling nauseous in a public setting, and the general feeling that you were universally insignificant.

Aaron's symptoms centered around the plain fact that he excelled at nothing, had no exceptional powers, and didn't have a single outstanding attribute. He was stuck in the middle of his class, in the middle of a town in the heart of the Midwest. Which might make you wonder, how could such an average teen ever amount to anything—especially a hero unlike any other?

In reality, the only marvelous thing about Aaron wasn't even about him—it was his grandfather...

His stories were amazing.

Aaron would stop over at Pap's house almost every day on his way home from school. He knew the way so well, he could just let his mind wander as he walked. Even when he was blocks away, he could make out Pap's house like a pinpoint between the large, shady trees. As he drew nearer, the house seemed to rise up out of the ground like a secret, hidden place that only Aaron could see.

The front door was never locked, and Pap could usually be found in the downstairs library, reading through the many volumes of his leather-bound books.

There was great comfort in the dark-brown woodwork along the hallway. Aaron anticipated making his way through the familiar corridor, to find Pap either sitting behind his desk or sifting through his shelves of books.

There was a standard ritual that had been created between Aaron and Pap. Aaron walked down the hall and yelled, "Pap, it's me!"

In return, Pap yelled from the next room, "Ahoy, my boy! Come in and see me!"

Aaron entered the library and Pap was there, in his favorite, houndstooth-upholstered chair. There was a cold bottle of root beer and some cheese and crackers set atop the side table as was the custom. A glass dish filled with peppermint candy laid off to the side for afterwards.

Aaron sat down in front of the old chair, grabbed his root beer, and waited for Pap to flip through the pages to one of his many stories. The old grandfather clock struck its chime at a quarter past the hour. That single, wonderful ring signaled the beginning of their daily ritual.

For Aaron, this was always the best time of the day. At that brief moment in time, Aaron sat in anticipation of what would come next. He never knew what the words would be that came from Pap's mouth. But what he did know was that they would be magical, wonderful, and take him on a journey far from the mundane streets of Oakville.

These were the thoughts that ran through Aaron's head as he stepped off the sidewalk and onto the front path of Pap's house. He'd really taken Pap's house for granted, even though Pap spoke about it with great pride.

It was a neat house on an old tree-lined street. As he approached the home, he never noticed the angled roof or the red bricks that led to the steps of the big front porch. Pap lived in one of those Sears Craftsman homes from over a hundred years ago. It was the kind you could order from a catalog with all the materials and plans included. Pap had bought the house from the original owners, who had built the home all by themselves.

But as Aaron approached the front porch, he still wasn't sure why the old house was so important to Pap. The weathered door handle in his hand felt as familiar as ever as he squeezed it slowly and leaned in with the usual amount of pressure.

The unlocked front door gave in with no resistance.

"Pap, it's me!" Aaron yelled, as was tradition. The teen waited for the standard response, but no answer came. So, Aaron yelled again, a bit louder this time, "Pap, it's me!"

As the echo from his voice faded, all that remained was the uneasy silence and the faint dust that floated through the afternoon sunbeams that danced across the hallway floor. This had never happened to Aaron before. His grandfather had always let him know when he'd be going out of town. On the days Pap was gone, Aaron knew to just head straight home. Pap would never leave his door unlocked when he wasn't around.

Something just didn't feel right as Aaron crept through the hallway toward the library door. For the first time in Pap's house, Aaron was scared.

His imagination ran wild with dark thoughts and crazy ideas as he peeked around the doorjamb. He half-expected to find Pap sprawled out on the floor—dead—perhaps murdered by some unseen intruder. Maybe the burglar was still hiding somewhere in the house, waiting for his next victim.

Aaron blurred his eyes on purpose, not wanting to see what might be lying by Pap's favorite chair. As he slowly allowed his vision to clear, the teen was able to focus on the chair, the table, the fireplace, and the shelves full of books. To his great relief, there wasn't any dead body to be found. The room was completely empty and looked like it had been untouched for days. As it was Monday, Aaron hadn't been to visit since Friday; so Pap could have gone somewhere over the weekend. He tried to comfort himself with logical thoughts like this, but he couldn't help the overriding feeling that something was terribly wrong.

The teen carefully made his way deeper into the library. He gently looked through the items on Pap's desk. After careful consideration of some loose papers and notes, Aaron decided that there was nothing of great interest there. He leafed through a few of his grandfather's books and found nothing. It seemed that Pap had left things just as they'd always been, as if he was still there.

Aaron left the library and began to check out the rest of the house. He wandered into the kitchen and the formal sitting room—no Pap. He ran upstairs and investigated each bedroom—no Pap. He even braved the gloomy basement that still frightened him a little—no Pap.

The dejected grandson gave up on finding his grandfather for now. Aaron looked everywhere and figured it was time to head home and tell his parents about Pap's disappearance. If Pap was really gone, someone needed to do something about it, quickly.

As he made his way through the front hallway toward the door, Aaron passed the library once more. He peeked in again, just to be sure that he hadn't missed anything. As his eyes surveyed the entire room and returned back to the hallway, he noticed something that he hadn't seen before. Lying on the floor, halfway between the library entrance and the front hallway, was a small piece of parchment paper.

The teen picked up the paper excitedly. There was something written on it. It was one word, scribbled in Pap's handwriting with black ink. The cursive letters were looped together with a long, dark ink trail at the end. They spelled:

Grandfather.

2
One Word

Aaron stared at the piece of paper. That one word, "Grandfather" pulsed right off the page he held in his hand. He knew what the word meant, but he couldn't figure what the word really *meant*. It didn't make any sense to him. He never called Pap "Grandfather." No one did. So why would Pap scribble a note with that name on it?

As the teen examined the parchment more closely, he wondered even more. It looked like Pap had scrawled this message in great haste, as if he'd run off somewhere quickly. Aaron's mind raced with all of the endless possibilities that were contained in that one little word, "Grandfather."

With some confusion and a bit of frustration, Aaron realized that he held a puzzle that wasn't going to be solved by standing inside Pap's house, letting his thoughts tumble around his skull. He needed to get home and talk to his mom and dad. Maybe they could help him figure out this mystery.

The walk home was quick and efficient—in fact, it wasn't a walk at all. It was a full-on sprint that left Aaron breathless and slightly sweaty as he finally slowed down in front of his own house. With little warning, Aaron burst through the back door and into the kitchen. He startled his mom so much that she dropped the dish she was carrying, and it crashed on the floor.

"Aaron Anthony Anderson!" his mom yelped, "you scared the wits out of me! What's the hurry now?"

"The big, bad bullies are probably chasing him again." Aaron's big brother, Marty, had slipped into the kitchen to raid the refrigerator. "You better get faster, or start working out, shrimp. Those goons are gonna catch up with you someday."

"Shut up, Marty," Aaron gasped, still winded from his frantic run home. "That's not what happened."

Aaron turned his attention back to his mother. "Sorry, Mom, it's just, I stopped at Pap's house ... He was gone!"

"What do you mean, gone? Like, he went out for a while?" his mother asked, trying to make sense out of the words coming from her deflated son's mouth.

"No! The door was unlocked; nobody was home. I looked all over the house for signs of him. Just when I was about to give up and come back here, I found this."

Aaron handed his mom the small piece of parchment with the word *Grandfather* written on it. Mrs. Anderson took it from her son and examined the piece of paper carefully. Other than the scribbled script that was so unlike Pap's normal handwriting, she couldn't figure out what the note meant.

"Where did you say you found this?" Aaron's mother questioned.

"I found it right outside his library, where he always sits waiting for me."

"Hmm," his mom thought out loud. "This is curious, but probably nothing to worry about. You know Pap—he's always heading out somewhere, God only knows where."

"Yeah, Mom, but when he does that, he always calls. He'd never leave without telling anyone... Something's wrong, I can feel it!"

Dad stepped into the room. "What's wrong?" he asked.

"Dad!" Aaron gripped his father's arm. "Pap's gone! That's what's wrong!"

Dad squinted. "Do you mean 'gone' like on one of his little trips, or is he actually missing?"

"We don't really know, dear." Mrs. Anderson's voice sounded pinched. "Aaron found a piece of paper outside of Pap's library that seems a little strange."

Aaron handed the paper to his dad so that he could get a better look at it. His dad took the small piece of parchment and looked it over carefully. Mr. Anderson held the paper up to the light, flipped it over a few times, and rubbed the dry ink back and forth with his thumb.

"I wonder why he would write *this* word down. It looks like he was in a hurry when he wrote it, that's for sure."

Aaron's dad handed the paper back to Aaron and sat down at the kitchen table with the rest of the family.

Aaron didn't notice that his father was staring at the newspaper, partially folded on the table in front of him. The headline read:

THREE FOUND DEAD UNDER MYSTERIOUS CIRCUMSTANCES

Those deaths were no accident. Aaron's dad knew more than he was willing to tell.

Mr. Anderson averted his gaze to hide his concern. After a moment of thought, he cleared his throat, "Well, I'll make a few phone calls to make sure that Pap is okay. He's been pulling crazy stunts like this since I was a kid. But I have to say, he's never left without telling anyone before… I think that's what bugs me the most."

Aaron looked back and forth between his mom and his dad. "So, what are we supposed to do while you check into things?"

Aaron saw the concern in his dad's eyes, "Son, I don't want you to do anything right now. Let Mom and me handle this for now. There is one thing you can do, though."

"What's that, Dad?" the teen asked hopefully.

"You can stay away from Pap's house until he returns. You did lock the door after you left, didn't you?"

"Sure, Dad, I locked everything up before I ran out. I didn't touch anything else while I was in there either."

"Good," his dad said reassuringly. "If I can't locate Pap by tomorrow, I'll have to get the police involved. And if that happens, they're not going to want a bunch of people rummaging through Pap's house before they get there. So, you just keep away from there until we've sorted these things out, okay?"

Aaron looked a little dejected, as he'd been hoping

that he'd be able to help search for Pap. Now he couldn't even go back to the house to look for more clues.

Aaron felt anxious, frustrated, and frightened. He wanted to do something, but what?

At this point, anything could have happened to Pap. He could have been kidnapped and was now being held hostage somewhere. Or he could have run away to some foreign country to get away from government spies. Aaron's mind raced with all of the endless, dangerous possibilities that could account for Pap's whereabouts. But in the end, it didn't matter, because he'd been told to do nothing.

After dinner, Aaron watched a little TV and tried to distract his rambling thoughts. Show after show passed across the television screen, but Aaron hardly noticed them. His mind tossed and turned like a tiny boat atop the rough, giant waves of an angry sea. The same questions circled around his head: Where was Pap? How long had he been gone? Why had he left that note? What was it supposed to mean?

The evening shadows continued to creep along the wall of Aaron's bedroom, as the moon shone eerily through the window. It was already late, but he couldn't get to sleep; his thoughts wouldn't let him. He knew that he'd promised his parents not to go back to Pap's house. But something was calling him back there. He didn't know why, but some invisible force was telling that he had to do exactly what he wasn't supposed to do. No matter how he tried to push the thoughts out of his head, they just crawled back in, even stronger than before.

It was the worst night of Aaron's entire life. The teen tossed and turned for hours with horrible visions of his lost grandfather, mysterious floating pieces of paper with unintelligible words on them, and a locked old house that held the dark, hidden secrets that he couldn't touch.

When the sun finally rose, Aaron had been awake for hours. The play between light and shadow on his bedroom wall was unsettling. The shadows seemed longer and the light dimmer than usual. He just wanted things to be normal again.

In fact, he had never been so happy to see another school day start. As he showered, dressed, and combed his hair, he reveled in the normal routine that made things seem a bit better than the day before.

Strangely enough, something else had happened as the night passed. As Aaron headed downstairs for breakfast, the swirling thoughts and confusion that he'd felt were gone. In their place was a feeling of nervous resolution. He was going to have to break his promise to his mom and dad. Even though he felt bad about doing it, he now knew that he *had* to go back to Pap's house.

It was like Pap was calling him to do it.

3
The Clock in the Library

School seemed darker than usual. Aaron couldn't explain it, but it was like a cold shadow hovered over everything. Aaron trudged through his classes like an old winter boot through heavy, slushy snow. It wasn't until he ran into his best friend, Jake, that Aaron was jostled out of his mental stupor.

"What are you doin'? Playin' Zombie Boy all day?" Jake asked Aaron as he bumped his friend with a playful elbow.

Jake Perez was a thickly built, black-haired teen, who also happened to suffer from the same Middleitis malady as Aaron. His symptoms were nearly the same as his best friend's, except for the fact that he came from the middle of a much larger family, and lived in a much smaller house on the edge of the nicer neighborhoods.

Jake was much more headstrong than Aaron. He had to be just to survive in a family with seven brothers and sisters. It was the kind of environment where the loudest gets heard and the quiet one disappears into nothingness. For Jake, every day was a fight against invisibility. It was a fight he fought alone—until Aaron.

They hadn't met until junior high school, where kids from all over the city were brought into a single building. Since then, they'd become inseparable. It may have been that Middleitis was all they had in common, but it was more than enough.

"Huh? What are you talkin' about?" Aaron asked with his head still in a fog.

Jake responded, "I said, are you planning on acting like a zombie all day, or what?"

"Uh, no, sorry, man, I've just got a lot on my mind right now."

"Like what?" Jake asked.

"Well, if you really want to know, I have to break a promise I made to my parents last night. By the end of the day, I'll be the biggest liar in the world."

"Don't be such a drama queen, Aaron—it couldn't be that bad." Jake jabbed Aaron lightly in the ribs to loosen his friend up a little. "What kind of promise are we talking about here?"

Aaron slid his back down the front of his locker until he was sitting directly on the floor. He stared up at Jake with a look that begged for help and understanding.

"You're the only one I can really trust with this." Aaron swallowed back his emotion. "My grandfather disappeared yesterday. No one knows where he went. I found a clue near his library door, but my mom and dad made me promise that I'd stay away from his house... But I have to do something."

Jake finished Aaron's thought. "And now you're gonna break your promise and go back, right?"

"Yeah," Aaron said defiantly. "It's like I don't have a choice. I feel like my grandfather is calling me—like he wants me to go back."

"So, you gonna do it?" Jake asked matter-of-factly.

"I'm goin' right after school," Aaron answered with renewed conviction.

"Well, I guess I'm goin' right after school too!" Jake replied with all of the excitement and energy that Aaron lacked.

"Really, you'd do that for me?"

"Sure," Jake said, "I mean, c'mon, I could use a little adventure in my life, you know?"

Slowly, but much surer of himself than before, Aaron got up from the floor and finished getting his books for his next class. Jake smacked him on the back with a supportive slap as they made their way down the hallway.

"In fact, let's skip the rest of the day," Jake suggested as they walked.

"You mean it?" Aaron hesitated.

"I'm in if you are," Jake smiled. "We're breaking rules and promises today, so what are a few more?"

Aaron grinned and nodded. The decision was made.

Both teens ducked quickly out of the building. Since Jake lived a little further away from the school than Aaron, he usually had his bike with him.

"Well, you ready to do this?" Jake asked Aaron as they stood by the bike rack, as if he was questioning his friend's resolve.

"I guess so," Aaron answered with less enthusiasm than Jake had hoped. "I feel crummy about lying to my mom and dad, but it's like I don't have any choice, you know?"

Jake smirked. "I get it, but that's not gonna stop us now; let's get goin'."

Jake sat on his bike but didn't pedal. He just pushed the bicycle along lightly with the tips of his toes as Aaron walked alongside of him. The conversation ghost-rode just like Jake's bike, as the teens avoided thinking about what they were about to do.

Pap's house was only a few blocks away from the school, so it didn't take long for the teens to reach the front walk of the old, tree-shadowed home. The sun was still out, but a faded moon slowly appeared out of the western sky.

A peculiar feeling came over Aaron as he set his left foot upon the walkway in front of Pap's porch. It was an uneasy sensation. Usually Pap's house was a place of comfort, a place where he felt safe, secure, and protected from the world outside. But that warmth had been replaced with a shadow over his soul. The air around him shifted with uncertainty, anxiety, and the growing sensation that his whole life would change when the door opened.

Jake got off his bike and pulled the kickstand down. "C'mon, man, what are you waiting for? Let's get inside before someone sees us."

Both teens made their way up to the front door. Aaron reached into one of the huge, potted plants that sat on either side of the door. He fumbled around the dirt for a minute until he victoriously lifted a shiny metal key from the giant plant.

Aaron turned the key in the lock, and tumblers released as the teen grasped the antique door handle. In one careful, creaking motion, he swung the house door open. Both teens entered the main hall as the door thunked shut behind them.

"Wow, your grandfather has a cool house," Jake pointed out as his eyes ran up and down the walls, halls, and windows that surrounded him. The house was filled with interesting artifacts, eclectic artwork, and ancient tapestries staged along dimly lit hallways and corridors. It felt like walking into a cool, old museum.

The clock in the library rang a quarter past the hour.

"So cool," Jake added.

"Yeah, it's pretty neat," Aaron muttered, fearing the worst.

At that moment, Aaron reached into his pocket and pulled out the scrap of paper that held the only clue he had. He stared at the stained ink as if the letters would magically reassemble into some new message that would make more sense. Then maybe he could figure out where Pap had gone.

"What's that?" Jake broke Aaron's trance, pointing to the piece of parchment in Aaron's hand.

"Oh, this is the note my pap left on the floor by the library," Aaron answered as he handed the paper over to his friend. "I had to steal it back from my dad when he wasn't looking."

"What do you think it means?" Jake wondered as he stared at the word "Grandfather" scrawled on the crumpled, yellowing paper.

"I wish I knew, man. I hope Pap's all right!" Aaron

said with a deep sigh. "That's why I had to come back here; I know it's a message for me."

Jake didn't say a word. He began to walk around the first floor of the house, looking at things differently now. Before, he'd had no idea what he was looking for. But now he tried to detect anything that might seem out of the ordinary, like maybe a phone left off the hook, or some knickknacks out of place, or even a broken vase or something. Maybe Pap had left another, secret sign that was out of plain sight.

After a few long minutes, Jake returned to the main hall, where Aaron was still looking. "Hey, you called your grandpa 'Pap,' didn't you?"

"Yeah, why?" Aaron answered slightly confused.

"Well, I was just wondering, why would he write down the word 'Grandfather' if you never called him that?"

Right at that moment, the ancient chime began its familiar toll, resonating in Aaron's ears.

A thought suddenly exploded in Aaron's head like an M-80 firecracker. He yelled out, "The clock!"

Aaron jumped up and grabbed his friend by the shoulder. The old tapestry rug rumpled under his feet as Aaron skidded across the hall into the library. "It's the grandfather clock! That's what he was talking about!"

Jake rushed in right behind Aaron, and both teens

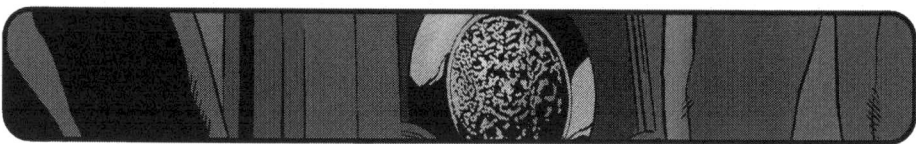

stood in front of the impressive grandfather clock that stood majestically in the corner of Pap's library.

Aaron noted, "Pap used to tell me to keep away from it. He said that it was a man-eating clock, filled with human bones. He never wanted me to touch it."

The massive clock was far older than both teens put together and just as tall. As their eyes climbed from the base of the clock cabinet up to the handsome handed face, Aaron and Jake were struck with a feeling that this was no ordinary timepiece.

"Do you think this is what 'Grandfather' meant?" Jake questioned.

"I'm sure of it," Aaron answered, with the first feeling of conviction that he'd felt since Pap disappeared.

The two teens continued to stare at the grand clock. They noticed the intricate scrollwork of the deep mahogany case, and the impressive brass weights and pendulum within the glass cabinet. Silver and gold accents had been etched into its metal flesh like tiny, elegant tattoos. Above the standard hands and numbers of hours and minutes hovered a separate, mysterious dial that managed the movement of a metal moon across the upper face of the clock. It floated between two globes and numbers set from 1 to 29—a lunar calendar.

Jake broke the silence, "What do you think he wanted us to do with the clock?"

"I'm not sure." Aaron continued to study the lunar dial. On it, the moon floated just below the number 15. That meant the lunar cycle was still in a full-moon phase. "I don't know why, but I think the moon has something to do with it."

With that, both teens leaned in closer to inspect the workings of the clock. Jake grabbed the cabinet doorknob and swung the glass door wide open. No sooner had he done that than the weights and pendulum lifted up, out of view, exposing a black velvet curtain that they hadn't noticed before.

With a slightly shaky hand, Aaron pushed the curtain aside. The teens leaned in carefully to see what was behind the curtain, while still keeping their feet firmly planted on the floor. An odd light shot through the library window. A distant whooshing sound could be heard, like the wind blowing through an underground cavern.

Then, before Aaron and Jake could react, before they could say anything, the once-distant wind whipped up from behind the black curtain and swallowed them whole.

The house was quiet once more.

The library was empty.

Aaron and Jake were gone.

4
Stories to Tell

Everything was spinning as Aaron and Jake were pulled through an invisible vortex of light and darkness. They had been sucked into some sort of hollow tube or tunnel that hurtled them deep into the unknown.

Prism colors pulsed around them as they flew without flying, fell without falling, and spun while standing still. What might have taken seconds seemed to take an eternity to end. But it did end, finally.

They landed with the same slight jerk that comes just before a large elevator comes to a complete stop. It was dark, and they seemed to be enclosed within a tiny, walled room.

Aaron groped around in the darkness, feeling for any latch, handle, or knob that might indicate a doorway of some kind. It didn't take long for Aaron to find an actual door with his hand, even though he couldn't see it.

"Hey, Jake," Aaron whispered, "I think I found a way out."

Aaron grabbed his friend by the arm and reached for the invisible doorknob with his other hand. Surprisingly, the door wasn't locked, and it opened with ease. What was not a surprise was the bright light that flooded Aaron's and Jake's eyes as they stepped out of the little room. Once the initial shock of brightness wore off, both teens focused on their surroundings.

It really wasn't what they'd expected at all. After being sucked into a giant clock, they'd half-expected to be in a land of fairies and elves or some otherworldly place. But they weren't in a place like that at all. In fact, as they looked around, they realized that they were standing in the hallway of a strange school building. And the room they'd landed in was actually a janitor's closet.

What made the place so strange was that it looked so familiar, yet something was a little off. The hallway was at a weird angle. The ceiling appeared higher than usual, and the windows along one side of the building shimmered with an unusual blue tint.

"Where the heck are we?" Jake whispered.

"Maybe a school?" Aaron answered. "Like no school that I've ever seen. Look at that!"

Aaron pointed to some large canisters mounted on the wall. As the teens looked around, they noticed a lot more things that told them that they were no longer in their own world. Light emanated from the floor instead of the ceiling. Different colored buttons and levers stuck out of the wall near each classroom door.

"I wonder why we're here?" Jake puzzled, still trying to figure out his surroundings.

"I don't know. Maybe my pap is around here somewhere. He wouldn't have left that note if he didn't want me to find him."

Aaron and Jake were just about to explore the school when noise rang out down the hallway. It sounded like an electronic warble, alerting anyone who was in earshot.

Within seconds, the once-quiet hall was swarming with noisy, bustling students scurrying to their next class.

As the teenagers made their way past, Aaron and Jake noticed that their clothes were different, in colors they had never seen before. Even their hairstyles weren't the same. It wasn't like these people were Martians or anything. It was more like Aaron and Jake had been dropped into another country, and they were the oddballs.

Both of them moved away from the lockers, then slipped through the crowded hallways, trying their best to blend in and disappear into the crowd.

Eventually, the students dispersed, and the halls were empty again. If Aaron and Jake had known what was going to happen next, they would have begged for the crowd to come back.

In the silence of the empty hallway, a cold wind blew, sending a shiver right through both teens. They looked down at the other end of the corridor, trying to understand what they were seeing.

There was more than one of them. They looked like dark masses of black smoke.

"What are those?" Jake asked nervously.

"I don't know, but they don't look friendly," Aaron replied, as his flesh prickled.

Whatever they were, their presence felt dark, sinister, and foreboding. Aaron and Jake wondered what to do next.

But before the teens could make up their minds, the shadowy entities made the decision for them. Without warning, the creatures accelerated toward Aaron and Jake, hell-bent to meet them head-on!

"Run!" Jake shouted.

Aaron didn't need to be told twice.

The two turned around and headed back the other way. Each time they looked over their shoulders, they could see the smoky wraiths gaining ground on them. Their lungs were burning.

"Faster!" Aaron shouted.

The shadows never slowed. In fact, they sped up, getting closer and closer to Aaron and Jake.

The teens made it to the end of the hall and turned the corner. The specters were right behind them, full of menace and evil.

"I can't run anymore," Aaron gasped, and he started to slow down.

"Don't stop!" Jake encouraged, as he pushed his friend forward.

But it was no use. The evil entities were nearly upon them.

That's right when it happened. A pair of unseen hands reached out from nowhere and yanked the teens into an empty classroom.

Jake jolted. "Hey, what gives?!"

Aaron tried to shake himself loose, when he noticed who those hands belonged to. Pap.

"It's you! Pap, it's you. I've been so worried."

Pap hugged Aaron hard. "Great to see you, my boy! Great to see you!"

For some reason, the creatures that pursued them continued down the hall, as if they didn't know their prey had disappeared.

Pap turned to Jake. "And who are you?"

"I'm Aaron's friend, Jake. Nice to finally meet you, sir," Jake gasped.

"The feeling is mutual," Johann Anderson replied. "And sir is not necessary, Pap will do just fine."

Aaron interrupted, "Pap, we were so worried about you. You just disappeared—and then you left that note on the floor by the library—and I didn't have any idea what it meant—and then we kinda figured it out—and then we both got sucked up into the clock!"

Aaron was completely out of breath with excitement and anxiety. Pap put his hand on his grandson's shoulder, "Whoa, now. Slow down, boy—take it easy.

Pap waved the boys over to a set of vacant desks that were away from the classroom door. He told them to sit down as he pulled up another chair and sat right next to them.

"Where are we?" Aaron asked first.

"And what were those things chasing us?" Jake added.

"Yeah," Aaron continued, "and what are you doing here?"

Pap took a deep breath and answered:

"You are in another dimension. Those creatures are Shadow People, and I am a Folkteller. I'm one of the few who must tell the stories that need to be heard."

Aaron and Jake were silent. They just sat there with blank faces, waiting for Pap's words to sink in.

"Oh, and I almost forgot," Pap said as he turned to Aaron. "You are my new apprentice!"

5
The First Trial

Aaron didn't know what to say. His head felt like one of those Magic 8 Balls that you shake and roll around in your hands until the answer to your question appears. It was shocking enough to get thrown into another dimension. But it was even more confusing to find he was supposed to be helping his grandfather do something he didn't understand.

Aaron didn't even have the chance to be thankful that he'd found Pap alive and well.

"What do you mean, *your apprentice?*" the boy asked dizzily.

Pap chuckled a little and patted Aaron gently on the back. "Nothing to worry about, my boy, nothing to worry about! I'll explain everything to you later, but for now, let's just say that you and Jake were brought here to help me out."

Aaron's grandfather briefly explained that he'd left

the note on the library floor on purpose, for Aaron to find. The teens had been brought to this new dimension by the Transit, a safe, secure dimension portal disguised as an old grandfather clock.

Pap went on, "You see, a Folkteller is someone whose job it is to tell stories that need to be told. This ain't a perfect world we live in, and Folktellers like me must remind people sometimes about why we're all here. Some people lose their way; I just try to help 'em find it. It's what I do. That's my job."

Just as Pap said these words, the classroom door flew open with a mighty crash. The old man and the two teens whipped their heads around to see who had thrown the door open. But when they looked over at the doorway, there was nothing there.

And then it happened.

Dark wisps of black smoke appeared in the open doorway. The darkness rose up from the floor and then separated into single, individual shapes that appeared almost human. But they weren't human. They had long bodies with arms, legs, and a head—but there was no face. These creatures were like solid black shadows.

Without warning, the black, faceless head of one of these shadowy forms snapped to the left so that it was looking directly at Aaron. The teen wanted to scream, but he couldn't. It probably wouldn't have mattered if

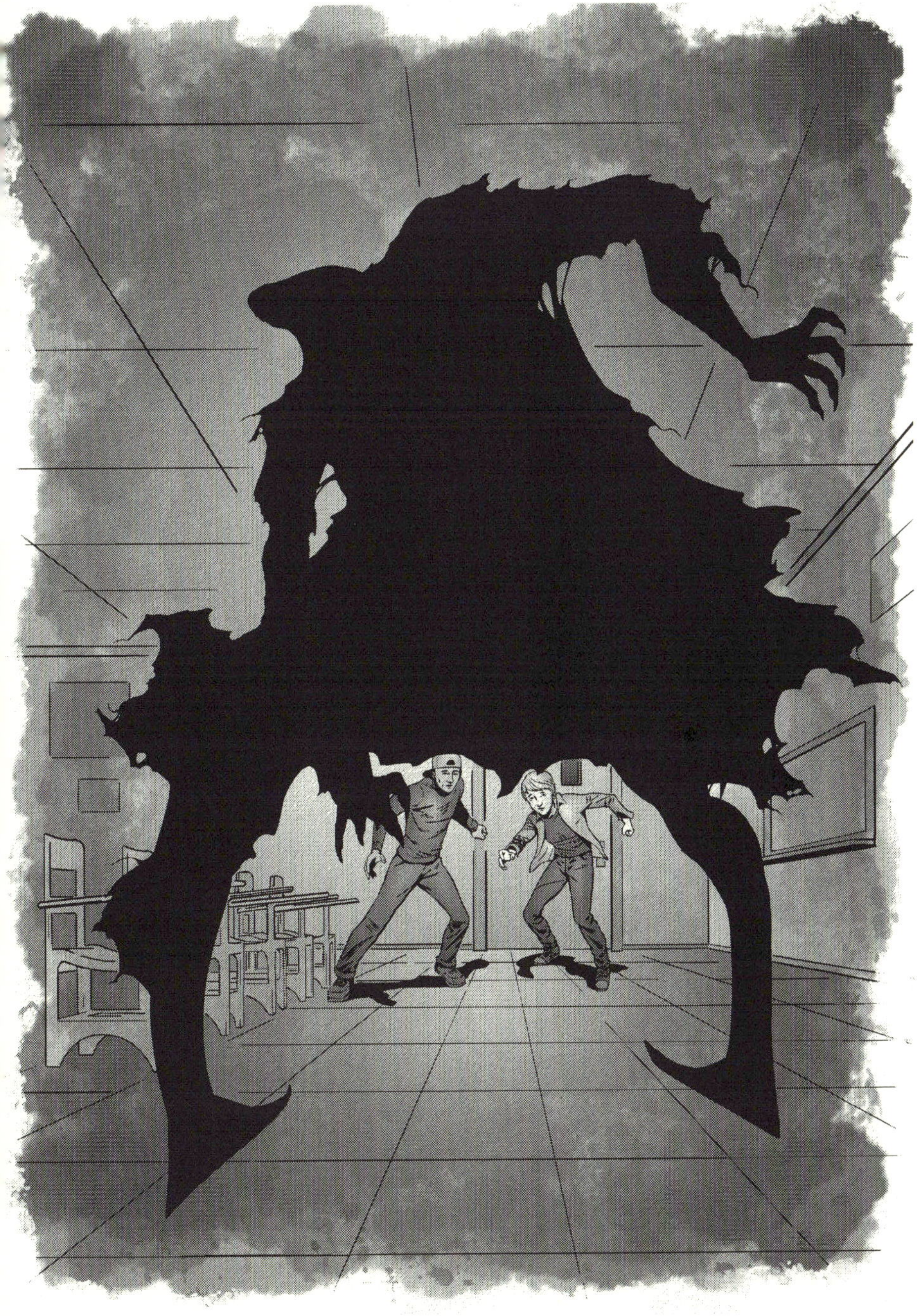

he had, as the creature began to advance on him with the most bizarre, jerking motion. It was almost as if it was stuck in two dimensions at the same time. It was like there was a strobe light on, and every time the light flashed, the creature's head and limbs were in a different position. The specter advanced on Aaron, contorting itself into different angles at every second. Eventually, this unnerving effect stopped, and the wraith appeared in its full shadowy form, advancing in a much more fluid motion now.

"Come with me!" Pap whispered roughly as he ushered the two toward the door in the back of the room. "They have trouble seeing us if we're moving."

The old man guided Aaron and Jake quickly out of the classroom and down the hall. While looking behind him the entire time, Pap moved his young wards into another room on the lower level of the building. Once he felt that they were safe again, Pap huddled close to the teens and continued his story.

Aaron wasn't really processing what his grandfather was telling him. He was preoccupied with the strange, scary black figures that had chased them out of the classroom.

"Pap, what were those things?" Aaron questioned intently.

"Like I told you before, those are Shadow People. No one is really quite sure what they are or where they come from. What we do know is that they've been following Folktellers for thousands of years, trying to stop us from telling our stories."

Jake had finally slowed his shaking down to a low tremor. All of the thoughts and questions that had been bubbling up inside of him were just starting to come out. "Pap, wh-why would these shadow creeps want to stop you from talking?"

The old man was quick and direct in his response. "Stories that won't be read must be told. I was sent here to tell a story to two people who really needed to hear one of my tales. The shadows want to stop me, plain and simple. We can talk more later, but for now you need to help me on my mission."

Aaron asked, "But Pap, how can we help? We don't know anything about all this storytelling stuff."

His grandfather answered, "For now, I just need you to distract the Shadow People while I tell my tale. In less than an hour, I'm slated to go to the school auditorium and give a speech. In that speech, I will tell a story. The story that I tell is meant to be heard by two very specific students who will be sitting in the audience. These individuals don't know it yet, but the story that they hear will have a great impact on them for years to come."

Jake questioned in a worried voice, "So how are we supposed to distract those shadowy things while you're telling stories?"

Aaron added, "Yeah, Pap, and why is the story only meant for those two kids?"

His grandfather pursed his lips and tried to figure out how to give the teens the answers they needed. "Firstly, Jake, I want you and Aaron to distract the Shadow People by drawing them into another part of the building. Once I begin my speech, they'll be powerless to stop me. And Aaron, the two people who need to hear my words are just kids now. But for the boy, this story will have a great impact on him in the future. The other child, a young girl, may be faced with some troubling choices in high school or college or even before. At some point in her life, my story may change the way she thinks—as well as alter the lives of those who are closest to her."

"Man, this storytelling is powerful stuff!" Jake said in awe.

"Indeed, it is," Pap replied. "And as important as anything in this world."

Just as he was finishing his explanation, long dark shadows appeared in the hallway like the cold shade of large trees planted only a few feet from each other. The teens shivered from the quick drop in temperature, and Pap's eyes narrowed in an intense gaze toward the hallway.

In a clear, quiet, and ominous tone, Pap declared, "They're here—and you must go."

Aaron grabbed Jake and they ran into the hallway on the second floor. The teenagers remembered what Pap had said about the Shadow People having trouble seeing you when you were moving. So, the teens ran past the three looming figures and then stopped—about twenty feet away. Once they stopped running, the three creatures seemed to turn their attention toward the teens. Their raggedy black velvet cloaks lifted off the floor and started to sweep slowly toward Aaron and Jake. As these inhuman beings drew closer, both teenagers felt a strange feeling come over them. It was a feeling like two magnets with opposite polarity being forced together by unseen hands. The teens' natural urge was to flee, but their feet seemed frozen to the spot where they stood. They were being pulled toward the creatures against their will. The Shadow People drew closer. Jake began to panic. He was finally able to unstick his feet from the floor and run, but Aaron grabbed his arm just before Jake flew off in the opposite direction.

"Jake, wait!" Aaron commanded. "Don't run yet. I have an idea. Let's let them get closer. Just before they get to us, we'll take off. That way we can draw them further and further away from Pap."

"Are you a lunatic?!" Jake shot back. "They'll kill us—or worse!"

"No, they won't," Aaron reassured him. "Something tells me that this will work."

Jake looked at Aaron and could see the confidence in his face. So, he nodded and turned back to stand next to his best friend. The dark creatures crept forward and now seemed zeroed in on the two teens. As they drew within a few feet of the boys, shadowy arms with elongated bladelike fingers reached out. It was as if they wanted to brush the soft faces of Aaron and Jake with their spidery hands.

It was right at the moment when those hands reached out that Aaron shouted, "Go, now!"

At his command, Jake followed Aaron in a mad dash down the hall. When they reached the end of the hall, they looked back. Far behind them were the three shadows, bobbing up and down in the distance like sinister buoys floating on some far-off waves. Eventually the dark creatures began to move forward again, making their way toward the teenagers once more. Aaron and Jake repeated their run-and-stop strategy as they continued to draw the Shadow People as far away from the auditorium as possible. The wraiths followed the teenagers all the way to other end of the school. As Aaron and Jake waited for the hovering shadows to catch up to them, they heard an announcement over the school's public-address system:

"Attention, all students: please report to the auditorium for our Monthly Speakers Assembly, which will begin in just a few minutes."

Within seconds the strange bell warbled again, and the hall was flooded with students. It was easy for the teens to blend in, even though they were still on the lookout for the Shadow People. And that was the oddest thing of all. The Shadow People had disappeared. They were nowhere to be found. The strange beings that had chased the teens around the entire school seemed to evaporate once that bell rang. Aaron and Jake couldn't figure it out. But as the students made their way to the auditorium, the teenagers decided that the best thing to do would be to follow them and listen to Pap's speech.

After all, traveling in groups was safer, and who knew where those shadows would pop up next.

6
A Story Told

The auditorium was packed. It felt like every student in the school had crammed into the seats, aisles, and open space within the room. The windows had been opened to let in some fresh air.

The weather outside was unlike anything Aaron and Jake had seen in their world. The air through an open window felt heavier, as if it wasn't made up of nitrogen, argon, oxygen and carbon dioxide, but some other unknown elements. The blue tint they'd noticed before came from a glowing star that looked like their own sun, but wrapped in cobalt cellophane.

Aaron and Jake managed to find a tight place in the back near the right side of the stage. The crowd was humming and buzzing like an agitated hive of active honeybees. Once the rear doors of the room closed, the principal walked out on stage.

"Good afternoon, students and faculty. I am very pleased to have such a large crowd here today. I am also very pleased to present to you our speaker of the month, Master Storyteller Johann Anderson!"

Pap walked out onto the stage with a bright smile, a nod of his head, and a friendly wave to the crowd. There was an energy in the crowd, one that might indicate the students were excited more to be out of class than by the presence of a potentially boring storyteller.

"Good day, my friends!" Pap spoke clearly into the microphone. "Would anyone like to hear a story today?"

A dead silence fell over the room. Pap took a deep breath. His eyes closed and he raised up his hands, as if he was a conductor, readying his orchestra. He fell into a trancelike state.

"Perhaps if I told you it was a story of life and death, love lost, love found, and a battle between the forces of good and evil? What if I shared with you a story filled with magical creatures who could travel time and space? Might you find that interesting?"

There was a silent pause from the crowd, followed by whoops and hollers, almost daring Pap to continue. One of the guidance counselors was pacing back and forth in the back of the auditorium, as if she was strangely aware of what was about to happen.

Aaron's grandfather began, "It all started once upon a time, many years ago…"

The entire auditorium went silent again. But this time it was a good silence: the kind of silence that clears the mind for something important, profound, and meaningful to enter the room. Everyone was drawn in by the words that rolled off of Pap's tongue. It was the oddest feeling that Aaron and Jake had ever felt. It was as if some sort of magical spell had been cast. The energy in the auditorium had shifted from boredom to anticipation, to intense interest. Pap's words were like strings of multicolored, blinking Christmas lights that the crowd watched in wonder and delight.

In the beginning, there was one singular force in the universe, known simply as the ONLY.
The ONLY was a creator, whose voice boomed with living Words.
The Words that the ONLY spoke were much more than just the Words that you and I know. No, these Words were extremely powerful. Once spoken, the Words became real.
That meant that when the ONLY said a Word like "tree," it became a real tree.
And when the ONLY said the Word "river," a flowing stream of water appeared, bubbling over the ground.
And when the ONLY said "lion," "tiger," or "zebra," a menagerie of animals populated the world in an instant.
So, it went that the ONLY created the oceans and the stars, the flora and the fauna, the heavens, and galaxies,

with the Words and a voice that rumbled with the power of creation.

And then the ONLY created people.

The ONLY used different Words to populate the world with many different kinds of people. They all lived in different lands, across many oceans: some in the north, some in the south, some in the far east, or even out west. And some lived smack-dab in the middle of everything.

But regardless of where the people lived, they all spoke the same language.

Once the universe was complete, the ONLY decided to share this power with some of the creatures.

The ONLY gave people the power to create, using Words. If they said "dog," or "apple," or "duck-billed platypus," one would surely appear, for everyone had the same power and used the same Words.

And it was right at that moment that trouble began in the universe...

Some people began to abuse the power to create. They used the Words the way you might use a well of unending wishes.

Many people created things that were beautiful, bright, and cherished by all those around them. They used their Words for the betterment of humanity.

But others used their Words for selfish reasons, gathering objects, trinkets, and baubles for themselves to hoard.

Still others used their Words to destroy—to crush and kill in order to control their environment.

And it was with these evil Words that darkness and shadow were permitted to enter this universe.

Over time, this misuse of power manifested a darkness so terrible that it had the power to overcome the very force that had brought it to life.

The ONLY saw what had happened and wept.

"They have abused the gift I've given them. Now something must be done, before it's too late."

So, the ONLY cast a spell upon the universe. This magic changed the power of the Word, splitting it in two, so that the Word became only a symbol of the thing it described—not the thing itself.

Now when someone said "turtledove," or "drawbridge," it was just a Word, a symbol of the thing, nothing else.

The ONLY cast one more spell. Suddenly the Words people spoke were different. Depending on where they lived, or what part of the universe they were in, their language differed greatly. Now the people couldn't understand what others were saying.

Confusion was everywhere. For a time, nothing was created, and nobody could understand why.

Darkness and shadow spread across the land and the seas, feeding on the chaos of a universe that had lost the ability to create and communicate.

The ONLY saw what had been done and sighed.

"They still have the power to create, but everything is different now. They'll have to rediscover the power for themselves."

So, the ONLY gave them the Story. The Story was the way that people could create again, and share with others. The Words would be spoken, written down, or drawn, or sculpted, or built into something tangible, until the thing that was created communicated the reality and the truth hidden within.

And from this fractured universe, new creators emerged. These were the people who understood what had happened to their universe. They were the ones who saw the spells of the ONLY and realized that it was only through their art and skill, that the pieces could be put back together.

So, they began to tell their stories. People from far and wide gathered to hear, see, and feel the new Words and images that told of the truth that had been lost so long ago. Stories were gathered, collected, and shared.

These weavers of stories were called by many names, but most came to know them as the Folktellers. They became the ones who traveled time, space, and dimension to tell people the stories they needed to hear. They were the collectors of legends and the tellers of tales, driven to share the light of truth and knowledge to keep their universe vibrant and alive.

And the shadows would follow them, seeking to control, command, and destroy the bearers of light. For to them the light was a terrible fire that burned right through them. It was a horrible force that they would never understand.

Yet they knew that the Folktellers' stories were formidable, and that those who wielded the Story held the power. So, the shadows sought to possess the very thing they feared the most. And so it remains to this very day. The struggle between light and dark, between shadow and illumination, continues, as the Folktellers share the storied flames of the light that guides the way, for all those who seek their own true destiny.

The crowd was mesmerized. But Jake and Aaron weren't. They were looking at the auditorium windows. They saw three Shadow People hovering right up against the glass. They looked like frustrated sparrows that kept flying into the pane without ever being able to pass through it. If the creatures hadn't been so scary, they would have appeared quite comical—three black balloons bumping up against the glass with dumb repetition.

Jake and Aaron wondered if anyone else could see what they were seeing. No one seemed to notice, as the crowd was completely entranced with Pap's story. But what the teens did notice was that the Shadow People were repelled by the same story that drew everyone else in. The story being told was acting like a force field that kept these shady figures at bay.

"Look, Jake." Aaron pointed at the window where the creatures continued to hover. "They can't get in... The story is keeping them out. That's what Pap meant when he said we'd be safe once he got started."

"You're right, man," Jake whispered. "And look over there. I bet those are the kids that this story is meant for."

Just a few rows away from the best friends, they could see one boy and one girl who seemed to be listening more intently than anyone. The boy was actually up on his knees, trying to get a better look at Pap as he told his story. The girl, who had been sitting with her legs folded and crossed underneath her, was now nearly standing. She craned her neck toward the stage like she was trying to capture every word that Pap spoke.

No one but Jake and Aaron noticed how intrigued both of those students were with Pap's story, but it was clear that something was happening within their heads. Aaron's grandfather finished his presentation to generous applause. The principal of the school thanked Johann Anderson for coming and dismissed the rest of students from the assembly. Just before the assembled students made their way out of the auditorium, Pap made eye contact with both Aaron and Jake. He waved them over to the side of the stage, behind the curtain.

"Boys, it looks like we accomplished what we needed to…," Pap whispered quickly. "Now we've got to make a hasty exit—come with me."

Aaron's grandfather guided his wards to a stage-door exit, away from the rest of the crowd. Their small group opened the door as quietly as they could and exited out into an empty hallway. They looked down at one end of the hallway. There was nobody there. Then they looked down at the other end of the hallway. Their blood ran cold. At the far end of the north hall, three Shadow People had spotted them and were now moving rapidly toward the Folkteller and his assistants. However, this time things were different. The Shadow People weren't moving slowly anymore. Now they seemed driven by some unseen force and had the speed of wingless deadly creatures.

"Look!" Jake yelled. "They've seen us!"

The leader of the ghoulish pack shot past the other specters and headed right for Jake. Before Jake could take another step, it was upon him.

Jake froze as the creature stretched out a half-formed form and grabbed him with its fingerless palm. A feeling of cold dread filled Jake to the brim, until he almost passed out.

Aaron didn't stop to think—he broke the beast's grip with a single swipe of his fist. As his hand cut through the shadow's clutch, the terror recoiled with a teakettle scream, and Aaron shared the same dread that passed through his friend's body.

Pap shoved both teens in the back and said firmly, "Let's go. We've got to get back to the janitor's closet—it's the only way home!"

All three of them bolted down the hall. The Shadow People sensed their movement and leaned forward in their flight, trying to build up speed and catch them before they reached the Transit in the janitor's closet. The chase was on as the small band of adventurers ducked around corners, scaled staircases, and slipped through empty classrooms in an effort to lose the trailing dark creatures. Just when they thought they had lost their ghostly pursuers, the Shadow People would appear closer than ever.

"They're gaining on us!" Jake yelled breathlessly.

"Keep running!" Pap yelled back with a wheezing in his chest. "We're almost there!"

They were about three classrooms away from the Transit when the Shadow People came within reach of Aaron. One of the specters nicked the heel of the boy's tennis shoe with its outstretched, spindly finger. That single touch almost sent Aaron flying head over heels onto the ceramic tile floor. He stumbled a little but maintained his balance long enough to keep running. It seemed like the grasping shadows would overtake the group before they could make it to the closet; there was no stopping these relentless creatures.

The rambling group was only one classroom away from the janitor's closet now. But the Shadow People were upon them, and their arms were outspread, as if they intended to wrap their prey up in the dark drapery of their hooded garments. Then, in a single spectacular moment, it happened. That girl, the one from the

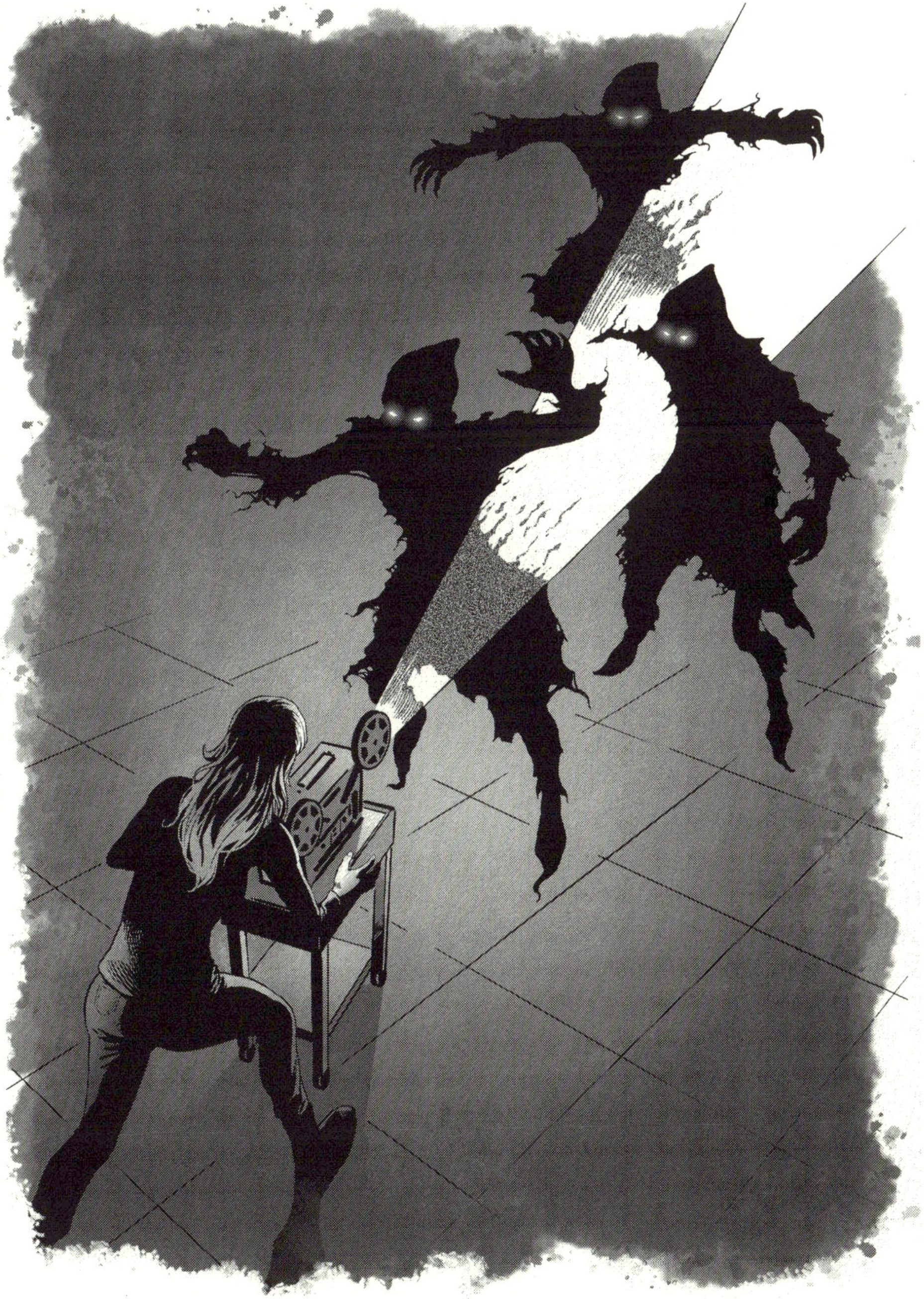

auditorium who had been listening so intently, stepped out into the hall. Her red hair flowed over her shoulders as she readjusted the crooked glasses on her nose. This was the same girl who had perked up more than anyone at Pap's story.

She was pushing an old film projector in front of her. The projector was already on and running as she pointed the lens toward the shadows. In an instant, the bright light from the projector shot through the three Shadow People like a lightning bolt through the dark night sky.

A shriek, a howl, and a wail echoed through the air as the floating horrors were slammed back against the far wall of the hallway. In the distance, Aaron noticed that three circles of light had created massive holes in the midsections of the creatures. They weren't dead, no, far from it. But the Shadow People had been severely stunned by the girl's quick thinking.

"Who was that?" Jake wondered as Aaron and Pap reached the closet.

"It was the girl, the girl from the assembly," Aaron answered with his last remaining breath. "Now get in the closet!"

Pap pushed the boys through the janitor's closet door and was just about to enter the room himself when he felt a slight tugging on his tweed sport coat. When he looked down, he saw the girl staring back up at him.

"I'm going with you," she stated, without wavering.

Pap knew that there was little time to argue, as the Shadow People could be up and after them again within seconds. So, without another thought, Pap nodded his head and ushered the girl into the closet. When the door closed, there was a flash of blue light, and Pap, Aaron, and Jake were sent spinning back to where their adventure first began, with an uninvited girl from another dimension squeezed in beside them.

2
The Nameless Girl

The Transit was not the most comfortable way to commute. It was usually reserved for a single traveler at a time. So the quarters were quite cramped as an additional three individuals tried to squeeze out of the central case of the grandfather clock. This became even more apparent as Aaron and Jake rolled out of the clock's cabinet and onto the library floor.

They were followed by the red-haired girl with the round glasses, who did a slight somersault, landing on her backside near Pap's broad mahogany desk. Lastly, Pap stuck his head out of the clock cabinet. He didn't roll or somersault or even cartwheel. He simply stepped gently out of the clock like he was leaving a familiar room.

"Well, that was quite a landing, wasn't it?" Pap commented as the teens were still regaining their balance.

Aaron and Jake managed to get to their feet. Jake

stuck out his hand to help the nameless girl up. She looked at Jake with a friendly yet firm face that refused his offer. Instead, she brushed off her knees and pulled herself up by one of the sturdy legs of Pap's desk.

Pap looked over at the rumpled crew and smiled with confidence and satisfaction. "Well, other than some bumps and bruises, it looks like no one is the worse for wear."

Aaron's grandfather then turned his attention to the girl. "My dear, I apologize wholeheartedly for our rudeness. We never got the chance to thank you for saving our skins. You arrived just in the nick of time."

"Oh, that's okay," the girl answered plainly. "It was something I just had to do."

"But how did you know?" Aaron interrupted. "How did you know where we'd be and what was going on?"

Aaron's grandfather put his hand on the boy's shoulder and gave him a slight squeeze. It was signal to Aaron that he needed to stop talking for a minute. Pap stopped the conversation momentarily. "I beg your pardon again, my dear. But we've been doubly rude now. I've failed to make proper introductions. You have no idea who we are, and we still don't know your name.

The girl smiled plainly. "Oh, that's easy—I'm Wendy, Wendy Perrault."

"Very pleased to meet you," Pap answered. "This is my grandson, Aaron Anderson, and his friend Jake Perez.

And I'm Johann Anderson—but most people just call me Pap."

Aaron looked at the girl with the long auburn hair and a few stray freckles dotting the front of her nose. Something about her seemed different. She didn't act like other girls he knew, especially the pretty ones. Maybe it was the fact that she even looked at him and said anything at all that impressed him.

Jake had a whole different perspective on the intriguing stranger. There was something in her smile, something in the way her eyes twinkled, that made Jake Perez feel like he was coming down with a wonderful flu. He thought that he might say something clever and witty, but every time he tried to talk, it felt like he was trying to re-swallow his own heart. The words would rise but never come out.

"Well, Wendy," Pap said, "now that we've been properly introduced, I'd like to know why you saved our skins from those Shadow People? Time is short, and I'm afraid the battle is just beginning."

Wendy turned to look at Pap, and for the first time, she really noticed him. He wasn't an old man, but he wasn't young either. His salt-and-pepper hair had a bit more salt than pepper in it. Along with a few weathered wrinkles, his face told her something about his age and wisdom. But his eyes, those twinkling blue eyes had all the sparkle and energy of someone much younger. To her,

Pap looked like a seasoned college professor who was still excited to shape the young minds of his students.

Wendy addressed Pap directly. "It was your story. Something in your story told me to follow you."

Aaron's grandfather smiled an uneven, quirky smile. He was puzzled and at a loss for words. How could his story have made such an immediate impact on her? It usually didn't work that way. Most of the time, a story took weeks, months, or even years to sink in. Pap was completely perplexed. This had never happened before.

"Wendy," Pap inquired, "what was it about my story that compelled you to follow us?"

Wendy didn't hesitate at all. Her voice was clear as a bell as she answered, "It was the parts about finding your destiny and the fight against the darkness. When I heard those things, something triggered inside me. It was a feeling that I needed to face the same thing. Right after that, I noticed Aaron and Jake looking over at me. So I just followed them. Like I said, it's like I was supposed to do it, like I didn't even have a choice. Then I saw those shadows chasing you. The first thing that I thought of was—*light makes shadows disappear.* I work in the AV room in my fourth hour, so I knew where the projectors were. And, well, you know what happened after that."

Jake and Aaron were riveted by Wendy's account of

the last few minutes before the Transit brought them back. Neither of them wanted to admit it, but they were impressed.

Pap had no problem recognizing Wendy's impressive talent and courage. "Miss Perrault, I can speak for all of us when I say that we owe you a great debt of gratitude. Your courage is uncanny!"

After Pap had finished thanking Wendy many times (a few too many times for the boys' liking), Aaron piped up. "So now what do we do, Pap?"

"What do you mean, 'do,' my boy? We've done so much already!"

"I mean, what are we gonna do about her? She doesn't belong here. How's she supposed to get back?" Aaron questioned as Jake nodded his head in support.

Pap cupped his chin with his right hand and thought for a moment. He then looked back at the grandfather clock. "Well, it seems to me that our guest will be here for a while, anyway. The Transit only stays open during the cycle of the full moon—and that time has now passed."

All the children looked intensely at the grandfather clock. Pap was right. The hand on the lunar dial had passed the number 15. That meant that the phase of the full moon was waning.

Jake ran over to the clock and opened the center cabinet. He rammed his head into the open space.

A muffled "ouch!" could be heard as his head met the wooden back of the solid clock's construction.

"I told you," Pap chuckled, "the tunnel is closed."

Jake sat on the floor in front of the great clock, rubbing the top of his head in an effort to ease the pain of the little lump that was forming near his crown. "That's one solid cabinet!" Jake affirmed.

Wendy giggled under her breath, not wanting to be rude. Aaron, however, had a look of great concern that spread across his face. His mouth looked like a crooked line scribbled above his chin.

"Won't people worry about Wendy?" Aaron wondered out loud. "If she has to wait for the next full moon, people are gonna wonder what happened to her."

Aaron's grandfather didn't seem worried at all. He gave Aaron a nod of confidence and assurance. "You're right to worry about Wendy, Aaron. But there's really no need to. You see, time is a funny thing, especially when you travel through it in extraordinary ways. The Transit has a strange effect on humans. When we return back through it, it's as if time hasn't passed at all. So, though time is always passing, sometimes it's not recorded or measured."

Jake finally got up and walked over to where everyone was sitting. "How can that be, Pap? We've been gone for hours. That's why the Transit is locked—'cause the full moon is over."

Pap put his hand on Jake's shoulder and pointed to

the face of the grandfather clock. "You're absolutely right, my boy, except for one thing. It's true; the moon phase is now a waning gibbous. But look at the hands of the clock. What time was it when you and Aaron took your unexpected trip into the Transit?"

Aaron, Wendy, and Jake all looked at the face of the grandfather clock. The hands read a quarter to four in the afternoon. Jake and Aaron had entered Pap's house after school at about 3:25 p.m. If they were to believe the clock, only twenty minutes had passed since they'd arrived at Pap's place.

"That's impossible!" Aaron shouted.

"Improbable, oh yes, but certainly not impossible," Pap responded. "It's like I said: time can do funny things, especially when other forces are involved. Think of it like reading a story. When you set the book down and stop reading, time in the story stops as well. The characters are frozen there until you pick the book up again."

"Okay, I get that, but what other forces are you talking about, Mr. Anderson?" Wendy asked politely but nervously.

Before Aaron's grandfather could answer her, there was a great shuddering throughout the house. It was as if the house felt a cold breeze and shivered with an overwhelming chill. Aaron noticed that his own breath began to fog. The temperature in the library must have dropped twenty degrees as the shiver ran through the house and over Aaron, Jake, Wendy, and Pap.

"I was afraid of this…" Pap said ominously.

"What other forces are you talking about, Mr. Anderson?" Wendy asked again.

"Afraid of what?" Jake asked with nervous intensity.

"It's the Shadow People… They're here."

"Pap, how could that be?" Aaron's voice cracked with tension and confusion. "Wendy blew a hole in them just before we got into the Transit!"

"Aaron, we don't have a lot of time. I'll explain more later. For now, know this—there are many Shadow People. They're everywhere throughout all time. They're attracted to Folktellers like us—even I don't fully understand why. Suffice it to say that I haven't told a story in this world since I left on my journey. That makes us all vulnerable."

"Is it the stories that keep them away?" Wendy wondered.

Johann Anderson waved off Wendy's question with a quick flip of his hand. He motioned the teens to sit down on the floor, as if they were preparing for a tornado drill at school. He ran over to his desk and pulled something large, brown, and leathery out of his bottom right-hand drawer. It seemed too little too late as the torsos and spindly legs of the Shadow People scraped the edges of the tapestry area rug, right where the three were sitting.

8
The Folkteller's Guidebook

Aaron, Jake, and Wendy looked around in horror. Long, dark arms and fingers began to protrude from the library walls. The Shadow People sifted through the doorway and bookshelves as if they were breaking the surface of a frigid lake.

Pap wielded the object that he had just pulled from a hidden compartment within the right-hand drawer. It was a very old leather-bound book with a discolored brass buckle on it. He opened the book quickly and began to read, as loud as he could:

Captain Jack sat around the campfire with his fellow pirates. He looked to his first mate and commanded him to tell them all a wondrous story of pirate adventures. The first mate obliged. He stood before his captain, his mates, and the roaring fire and began his story:

"Once upon a time, there was a captain surrounded by his fellow mates, sitting around a roaring campfire. The captain looked to his first mate and commanded him to tell them all a wondrous story of pirate adventures. The first mate obliged. He stood before his captain, his mates, and the roaring fire and began his story…"

Pap kept reading the story out loud, and the words looped and wound around the entire room.

Aaron, Jake, and Wendy had no idea what was going on. Pap's voice was so clear and strong, but not one of them had any idea what he was saying. They could tell it was a story of some kind, but they were too frightened to really listen. They were more mesmerized by the tone in which Pap was chanting the words from the book. It seemed he was casting a spell with an incantation read directly from the great leather book.

The Shadow People that had been closing in on the small band of adventurers froze in their tracks. An invisible force field had surrounded Pap, Aaron, Jake, and Wendy. The Shadow People were slowly being forced back through the walls, through the bookcases, and out of the library doors. As these creatures receded back to the darkness, they seemed to ooze blackness.

The children watched in amazement as their threatening attackers were pushed back out of sight. The frigid

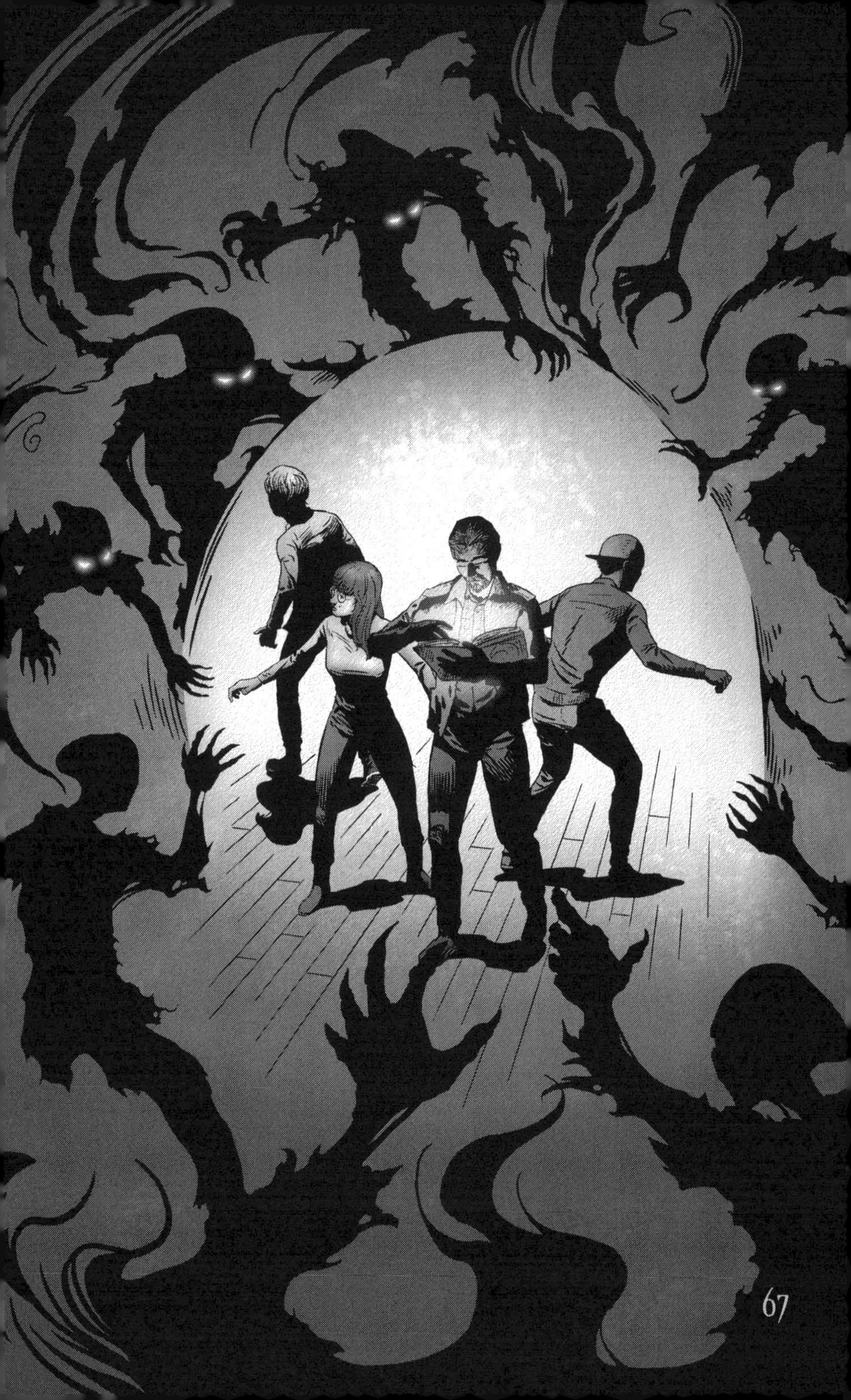

house relaxed and returned to its normal room temperature. Just as quickly as the attack had happened—it stopped. Now there was just an eerie silence and calm that resonated throughout the house.

Johann Anderson closed the book gently, listening for the soft click of locking clasp that wrapped around the entire book. He then produced a small key from his pocket, securing the secrets within.

"What the heck just happened?!" Jake yelped in confusion. "I—I thought we were goners for sure!"

"Pap, what did you just do?" Aaron demanded.

Beads of sweat ran down Johann Anderson's face. He shoved his desk chair out into the middle of the room and flopped down on it.

"That was too close…," he murmured under his breath as his arms draped over the sides of his leather chair. "I'm getting too old for this nonsense…"

Aaron, Jake, and Wendy were still sitting on the floor, staring at the old man, who looked like a Popsicle that had been left out in the sun for too long. They were all in a state of shock, still unclear as to what had just happened. The teenagers continued peppering Aaron's grandfather with questions. He held up his hand as if to shelter himself from the barrage of inquiries being hurled in his direction. It took Pap longer than a moment to regain his composure. But when he did, he was finally able to explain the actions he'd just taken:

"I keep forgetting how much you don't know about what I do. That's my fault. What just happened was my fault too… I'm so sorry. You see, part of my job is to tell stories on a regular basis. It keeps things in balance. Normally, that's no problem, as Aaron can attest—we share stories almost every day after school. But in my traveling, I was away much longer than I expected. That's what gave the Shadow People their power."

"Mr. Anderson, none of this makes sense to me," Wendy stated clearly. "So, your stories keep the shadows at bay?"

"Precisely, my dear." Pap's eyes seemed tired.

"Then what was that story you were chanting from the book you grabbed from your desk?" Jake chimed in.

"Oh, well, that story is an old Folkteller's trick," Pap responded. "It's a never-ending story. It has the properties within its text to repel even the darkest shadows for days on end. But it must be spoken word for word. That's why I needed the book."

"Okay, Pap, I was following you for a minute, but you lost me again," Aaron said with growing frustration.

"The story, my boy, never ends. If you listen to it, it becomes a story within a story that's within another story. When I tell it, the shadows are forced away for an extended period of time. It has the power of a single story multiplied by a thousand. Eventually the reverberating effect of the story fades and the Shadow People come back to their senses. That's why, as a Folkteller, I must constantly keep the stories alive."

Aaron got up slowly and walked over to Pap's desk. He picked up the heavy, old leather book and brought it over to his grandfather.

"Careful, Aaron."

"This is a special book, isn't it, Pap?"

Aaron held it cautiously in his hands, admiring the well-worn, gilded binding. His fingertips tingled as he stroked an old brass buckle and strap, noticing a tiny lock that held the entire volume together.

"This is the most important book I have in the world," Pap said solemnly. "It's the Folkteller's Guidebook."

Aaron handed the book to Pap. Instinctively, Aaron, Wendy, and Jake gathered around the old man's chair. They could barely make out the letters Folkteller's

Guidebook, in faded gold, right next to the name Johann Anderson. Pap released the clasp with an intricate key he kept in his vest pocket. As he opened the book, the three could all hear the binding creak, like a hidden, mysterious door was being opened.

The only words on the first page were written by hand. They read:

Stories that dare not be read must be told.

Aaron felt a shiver run down his spine. It was like those words were alive. It was as if that one simple sentence had been absorbed through his eyes and into his heart. Now the words permeated his brain and were branded on his soul. Aaron took another deep breath. Pap looked over quietly at Aaron, knowing what had just happened.

Aaron's grandfather gave his grandson a smile unlike any Aaron had seen before. "You really are my apprentice now."

Jake and Wendy were unaware of the magic that had just been transferred from the Folkteller's Guidebook into Aaron's heart. They were more curious about the contents of the old book.

"Pap, can we see more of what's in here?" Jake asked anxiously.

"I probably shouldn't have shown you this at all," Pap said thoughtfully. "There are only a few of these books in existence, and its contents are to remain quite secret. This was an emergency—that was the only reason you saw what you saw."

Pap ran his fingers across the face of some of the pages. It was hard to tell if he was reading with his eyes or with the tips of his fingers, like a blind person would read a braille book. But it was clear that whatever he was reading was deep and powerful.

Johann Anderson stood up slowly and walked back to his desk. He placed the book back into its special drawer. He then took out the small key he had returned to his pocket and locked the book's clasp securely. "My friends, as you've probably guessed, this is a book I use in my trade. Its secrets are not mine to tell, as its authors have sworn all future Folktellers to an oath of silence about its contents. Now, let's move on. We have other things to attend to…"

Pap was right. They still hadn't figured out what they were going to do with Wendy. They still had to wait almost a month until the return of the full moon. What were they going to do with this girl from another world until then?

Cousin Wendy

There was a light knock on the front door that made the small band of adventurers jump. The door creaked open, and Pap could hear footsteps moving into the front hallway.

Cautiously, Johann Anderson peeked around the library door. Below his own head peeked the heads of Aaron, Jake, and Wendy like a wary, curious totem pole.

"Dad?! Aaron?! Is anyone home?" came loud voices from the front hall.

"Mom! Dad!" Aaron yelled back as he ran out of the library toward them. He hugged both of them as if he hadn't seen them for days. His mom and dad were a little surprised at their son's unusual display of affection, but they were quite happy to see him.

"How did you know we—uh—*I* was here?" Aaron corrected himself feebly.

"Well, son," his dad replied through his gritted teeth, "when we told you not to come back here, we thought that the temptation might be too great. When you didn't show up after school, we just guessed that you might be here. I can't say that I'm not upset with you—what you did was stupid!"

"Your father's right...," his mom said, shaking her head at Aaron.

"Sorry, Mom...sorry, Dad..." Aaron said sheepishly.

It was at that moment that Johann Anderson stepped out of the library and into the main hallway. "Well, this is quite a family reunion, isn't it?"

"Pap!" Aaron's mom shouted as she ran over and hugged the old man. "I'm so glad you're safe. So glad..."

Aaron's dad walked down the hall and met his father

in front of the library doorway. "Really glad you're okay, Dad, really…" Aaron's dad gave his own father a sincere hug and a few thoughtful slaps on the back. "You had us all worried sick, you know."

Pap shooed his overemotional visitors back and looked a little disgusted. "What's all the fuss? I've done this trip more times than I care to count. Now, all of the sudden, everyone is worried about poor old Pap? Jeez Louise, you'd have thought I came back from the dead!"

It was kind of bizarre. Pap always spoke so clearly and properly. But when he got emotional, he'd revert back to his southern roots, and his voice would twang and bounce like the strings on an old banjo.

"Now, Dad, this time was different and you know it." Aaron's father stated firmly. "You'd never been gone that long, and then there was that cryptic note you left. What were we supposed to think?"

While all of the bickering was going on, Aaron was listening intently. For the first time, he realized that his parents were in on Pap's secret life as a Folkteller.

"Wait a minute," Aaron interrupted. "You mean to tell me that you guys knew all along? You knew about Pap and all of his travels and stories and books and stuff?"

"Well, of course we did, Aaron. He is *my* father, you know."

"So how come you never told me?" Aaron questioned with an injured, slightly angry tone in his voice.

Aaron's mom pulled her son closer to her own face. "Listen, honey, we knew that you'd find out soon enough. In fact, we were going to tell you on your next birthday, but it seems someone beat us to it."

"Don't go blamin' *me* now!" Pap scolded. "I just found out before my trip that the boy was going to follow in my footsteps. I was gonna talk to you both first, and then the shadows came. I was just lucky that Aaron and Jake figured out my note. I would've been a goner for sure!"

Aaron's mom and dad went silent. They looked at each other, wondering if they had heard Pap right.

"Y-you mean, he's one too?" they seemed to ask in unison.

"Sure enough," Aaron's grandfather said with conviction. "Aaron's a Folkteller, and he's my new apprentice."

"But Pap, how can that be?" Aaron's mom wondered out loud. She looked over at her husband and added, "Jason is your own son, and he's not a Folkteller. In fact, he's one of the worst storytellers I know. Even when he tells a joke, he ruins the punch line."

"Gee, thanks for the vote of confidence, dear." Aaron's dad mumbled.

"Oh, honey, you know what I mean. I love you, but you're no Folkteller."

"Okay, I think everyone gets the point, Ana." Jason

motioned to his wife to change the subject. "So, what about it, Dad? How did Aaron suddenly become imbued with all the powers of a Folkteller?"

"How in Hades should I know?" Pap answered curtly. "It's the higher powers that make these decisions, not me. They just send down the word and I do what I'm told. Besides, these aren't decisions that you question. It's my job to uphold the order, and that's what I intend to do. Aaron's been made my apprentice, and I'll teach him everything I know. And don't forget, he's just an apprentice—he's got a lot to learn before he becomes a full-fledged Folkteller."

Everyone was still standing in the hall by the library as they bickered back and forth. Aaron's parents didn't even notice the strange girl who had been standing right behind Pap the entire time.

"Jason, Ana." Pap's tone became much calmer and gentler. "I'm sorry for not talking to you sooner about this. I was about to tell you when I got—well, when I got called away suddenly. Which brings us up to the here and now. We'll sort all of this out, I promise. But for now, we have a more pressing issue."

With that, Aaron's grandfather stepped aside to reveal the young girl who had been hidden behind him. Wendy slid out from behind Pap into the full gaze of the small crowd.

"Hi, everyone." Wendy hunched her shoulders a little and wiggled the fingers on her right hand in a half-hearted attempted to wave. She wasn't shy; she just hated having to introduce herself, especially to someone else's parents.

Aaron's mom smiled and beamed at the young girl. "Well, who do we have here? Nice to meet you. I'm Mrs. Anderson."

"Hi, Mrs. Anderson. I'm Wendy… Wendy Perrault."

Pap didn't wait for any further introductions. "Our new friend Wendy was directly responsible for saving our skins and letting us get back to the Transit. It was her quick thinking that allowed us to escape the Shadow People."

"It really wasn't a big deal," Wendy said modestly. "I just shined some light on them and they disappeared."

"You're far too modest," Pap added. "Those creatures would have had us for sure if it hadn't been for your quick thinking. Using an old projector to pierce their dark hearts—it was genius!"

"So, how did she get here?" Aaron's dad wondered out loud.

Jake stepped up and inserted himself into the conversation. "She followed us into the Transit and we all rolled out onto the library floor. We were only here for a few minutes when more Shadow People showed up.

Then Pap pulled out a book and read something to drive them away."

"The never-ending story?" Aaron's dad questioned quickly.

Pap nodded his head with a look of grave seriousness. Aaron's dad knew how serious it was. He knew that the never-ending story was not something to be used lightly. In fact, it was strictly forbidden for any Folkteller to use the story unless they were in imminent danger. Ana and Jason knew this too, which made them worry even more about Aaron and his new role as a Folkteller's apprentice. The danger of the never-ending story was this: if spoken aloud too often, it could create a loop in time, where everything would repeat and repeat and repeat itself for eternity.

But nobody was really thinking about that now. Aaron's mom and dad were more concerned with the bold girl they'd just met. Ana went over to Wendy and asked, "So where are you from, honey?"

"Um, I'm from Walnut Creek, in California." As Wendy answered the simple question, she realized that she had no idea where she was. For all she knew, she could have landed in a library in a house on the moon! "Uh, could you tell me where I am?"

"Why, you're in Oakville, Michigan," Ana answered.

Aaron's dad watched Wendy squirm a little. He could

tell that she was confused. In her mind, she was trying to figure out how the Transit had shot her all the way to Michigan in just a few seconds. Then, for no apparent reason, Aaron's father asked Wendy, "So, do you know what the date is?"

The girl cocked her head sideways, wondering why Mr. Anderson would ask such an odd question. "Why, it's seven in the third quarter of the metric year eleven. Why would you ask that?"

"What did you just say?" Pap needed to confirm what he thought he'd just heard.

Wendy repeated, "I said, it's seven in the third quarter of the metric year eleven."

Everyone went silent.

Jake was the first to break the uncomfortable quiet. "What the heck is a Metric Year? It's a Thursday in October, for gosh sakes!"

Aaron's mom shushed Jake and drew closer to Wendy. She asked in a calm, motherly tone, "Honey, can you tell me who the president is?"

Wendy answered just as quickly as she had answered the first question, "It's Janet Simmons—she's been our president for the last year or so."

Now everyone knew that she was completely wrong. The president of the United States was Wilson J. Solomon. He was already in his second term of office.

Wendy could tell that people were responding to her strangely. She began to get very uncomfortable.

"I don't understand what's going on," Wendy worried. "I thought I knew where I was, but now I'm not so sure…"

"Don't worry, sweetie." Ana tried to comfort the confused girl. "I'm sure there's a proper explanation for all this."

Aaron's grandfather had been listening very intently to the conversation that had just taken place. He pursed his thin lips and stroked his chin with the thumb and forefinger of his right hand. That meant that he was really thinking about something. After a few minutes, he interrupted Wendy's interrogation.

"I think I have a clue as to what's going on here. I can't be too sure, as I've never had company with me through the Transit. Usually, when I travel alone, I'm taken to places within my own jurisdiction, my own time period. Naturally, I assumed this was the case when we ended up at that school. Everything seemed normal—seemed perfectly ordinary to me—except for the Shadow People."

Pap took a few deep breaths and stroked his chin some more before continuing. "But I think we may have all just come from a parallel dimension. Even though Wendy's world looks a lot like this one, there appear to be some significant differences."

Aaron broke in. "But she talks just like us and her clothes aren't too weird or anything. I don't get it!"

"Well, Aaron," Pap said slowly, "I told you, time is a funny thing. It's not a straight line, and it doesn't always act the way we think it will act. I'm just as confused as you are."

Wendy looked even more worried now. In fact, she looked as if she was going to cry. "Does that mean I'll never be able to get back again?"

"Not to worry, my child, not to worry!" Pap said, trying to be reassuring. "The Transit will reopen in a few weeks, and I'm sure that will put you back right where you belong."

Of course, Johann Anderson wasn't sure at all. He did his best to fake a positive, cheery demeanor. But he really had no idea if the Transit would open the way it usually did. He knew that the Transit was the safest way to travel across dimensions, and wouldn't risk any other option.

Everything seemed so topsy-turvy right now that the Folkteller couldn't be sure of anything.

It was at that moment that Aaron's mom took control of the situation. She could see that everyone was becoming more nervous, confused, and upset by the minute. Her instincts were right, of course. You could feel the anxiety growing in the hallway.

Ana stepped into the center of the discussion. "Well, I'm sure that there'll be enough time to sort this out later. In the meantime, I think that Wendy should stay with us."

Aaron's father looked at his wife. He agreed without saying a word. It was Aaron who put up the biggest fuss.

"Why does she have to stay with us? Pap's got enough room right here."

"Not another word, Aaron. Wendy will be our guest. And when you bring her to school, you can just tell people that's she's your cousin."

"School?" Aaron was in shock. "Now I've got to bring her to school with me?"

Jake put his hand his friend's shaky shoulder. "Listen, man, relax. It's not a big deal, and it's only for a few weeks."

Jake had to be kidding. Aaron realized that his friend was wrong, and it was going to be awkward. Having Wendy at his house was a big deal. He dreaded the thought of having to share a bathroom, or of Wendy seeing his underwear in the laundry pile, or something worse.

But it didn't matter. Aaron just needed to deal with it. And what he still needed to deal with was the fact that he was a Folkteller's apprentice—and he had no idea what that really meant.

10
The Shadow Realm

It was a place where there was only enough light to reveal how dark it was. There was no sun; there was no moon—not a single source of illumination.

Most people would say that it was black as night, but the Shadow People knew better. They knew that there were varying shades of darkness, for without them, they would be unable to discern themselves from the others sliding and slithering about in their world between dimensions. To them, light wasn't light at all. It was only the absence of darkness that created uncomfortable gaps and spaces in the infinite shadows of their unrevealing world.

The Shadow People very rarely gathered together. They were solitary creatures that traveled in packs out of necessity, not out of any desire for companionship or socialization. They had gathered for one specific reason—to discuss their failure in stopping the Folkteller.

The peculiar thing was that Shadow People never spoke. There really wasn't any discussion at all. Their ability to communicate was telepathic. They could intuitively read each other's thoughts, so there was no need to talk, chat, or discuss anything. But still they gathered. These phantasms huddled together in a silent exchange of thoughts, frustrations, and strategies as to what they were going to do next. Thousands of years had passed, maybe even millions, since these lightless specters had first shadowed humankind. No one really knew, since Shadow People existed outside of time itself and could travel through myriad universes as if through doorways in a cosmic house.

Their only limitation was that each Shadow Person was stuck on a single path in a particular dimension. Though they could all gather in the Shadow Realm, only a small cluster could form in a specific dimension. Unlike Folktellers, Shadow People couldn't travel across dimensions. This was a constant source of frustration for them. This was their hell.

But now, for some reason, these murky wraiths had gathered with a new purpose. Together, they discussed their growing displeasure with the Folktellers across time. They were looking for a weak link in the chain of storytellers that had held them at bay for millennia. Perhaps the time was approaching when the transition between an old Folkteller and a new apprentice would afford them an opportunity to gain the advantage they sought.

They had targeted Pap and Aaron. To them, Pap wasn't a Folkteller and Aaron wasn't an apprentice. They had different names for these humans. They were called "Keeper" and "Flesh." Pap was seen as the keeper of the Folktellers' secrets and their power. Aaron was the young, vulnerable student, who appeared to them as easy prey: like the pink, soft skin of a young, innocent animal.

It was the book they were after. Perhaps the time was approaching where they might capture the one thing that prevented them from overtaking humanity. It was as old as the Folktellers themselves and was their greatest weapon against the darkness. Every Folkteller had one, but the Shadow People only needed a single copy to begin to tap into its power.

The Shadow People didn't call it that, though. They had no concept of books or reading or words. To them, the book represented the cause of their pain and suffering. It was an instrument of torture to these otherworldly apparitions. It was the light that melted their realm of shadows. They called it the Burning.

The Shadow People gathered in angry, terrible silence, wondering what to do next. It was critical that they take action before Flesh learned too much about the craft of the Keeper. There was only a small window of time before the student grew into a full-blown keeper of the truth. These obsidian dwellers were determined to act now.

Aaron was the Folkteller they feared most, and they had to do something before the teen discovered his true destiny.

They would steal the Burning and destroy it—and all the Folktellers along with it.

11
A Different School

Even though school had been in session for over a month, it was Wendy's first day in her new school. This situation was temporary, but that didn't stop Wendy from worrying about her clothes and makeup and how everyone would look at her. She just wanted to fit in.

As Aaron dropped her off at her new locker, Wendy was perplexed. "How do I open this thing?" Wendy wondered out loud. "These lockers are different than the ones I'm used to."

Aaron looked at her like she was nuts or something. "What do you mean, 'How do I open it?' They gave you a lock combination—just turn the dial to the right number and it'll open. Jeez!"

"I have no idea what you're talking about—I've never seen a lock like this before!" Wendy's temper was starting to get the better of her. Aaron hadn't exactly been a welcoming host since Wendy fell out of the grandfather clock from a parallel dimension. And now she was in a strange school, in a strange town, and she'd had just about enough of Aaron's bad attitude. "Listen, I didn't ask to come to school with you; it was your parents' idea. But I'm here now, and there are some strange things that I've never seen before. I need your help. If you don't want to help me—fine. I'll find someone else who can be a little less of a jerk than you're being!" Wendy stared at Aaron, who was just standing there like a little puppy who'd just gotten yelled at for chewing up his master's leather slipper. "Well, are you gonna help me or not?"

"Um, yeah, sure," Aaron mumbled humbly.

The school day went a little smoother after that. Wendy and Aaron never verbally agreed to back off, but it was clear that they had each decided to try a bit harder to get along.

Wendy didn't have any classes with Aaron, but Jake was in at least two of her classes, which made things a little easier. The hardest part of the entire day was dealing with the many things that were different from Wendy's world. Where Wendy came from, books were read not only by sight, but touch as well. They only had one schoolbook in Wendy's world. As they went to each class, the text in the book would convert into the appropriate lesson for that day. She wasn't used to carrying around so many schoolbooks—it seemed kind of silly to her.

There were other strange things in the building itself. Wendy had never seen a drinking fountain before. She watched in awe and amazement as the students would press a button and drink from the stream of water that shot out of the top of the odd contraption. In her school, water canisters were mounted on the outside of each classroom. Everyone could refill their own personal water container whenever they wanted.

When no one was looking, Wendy took a chance and went over to try to get some water for herself. She pushed the button and leaned in, only to get a faceful of water and a soaking wet shirt. She blushed as a few teenagers walked past, laughing quietly at her unhappy accident.

When the final school bell rang, no one was happier than Wendy to see the first day come to an end. Jake was in her last class and walked out with her.

"So, Wendy, how did it go today?" Jake asked as they made their way into the hall.

"Um, let's just say it was interesting…"

"What do you mean?" Jake had no idea what she was talking about.

"I mean, this world is a lot different than where I come from. On the surface, everything looks the same. But the more time I spend here, the more I realize that there's a lot that's completely weird to me."

"Yeah," Jake confirmed, "I know where you're coming from. School's hard enough without a bunch of strange stuff you've never seen before. I thought you were pretty gutsy before when you saved us from those shadow freaks. But coming to a strange school in another dimension? Now that takes real guts!"

Wendy smiled a smile like she had never smiled before. "Gee, thanks, Jake. That's the nicest thing anyone has said to me since I got here."

Jake's skin suddenly flushed red. His eyes darted to the other side of the hallway in an awkward effort to deflect Wendy's appreciation away from his blushing cheeks.

"Uh, um, let's get our stuff and find Aaron. Maybe we can go get something to eat after that—I mean, if you're hungry."

"Sure, I'd like that," Wendy said sweetly. "I'd love to have some curdwhups."

"Curdwhups?" Jake furrowed his brow.

Wendy explained, "You know, it's a sliced potato, deep fried and wrapped in a cheesy pastry. You can get them at Curdies—don't you have those restaurants here?"

"Hate to say it, Wendy, but there are no curdwhups or Curdies here in our world. Would you settle for some french fries from McDoodles?"

Wendy smiled, "Yes, I'd love that."

Slowly but surely, the day that Wendy had wished would end abruptly began to change. In fact, she wasn't so sure that she wanted to wish the day away anymore.

Life is weird like that. What begins as a day that seems quite miserable and unwanted can end better than anyone would have wished, guessed, or even imagined. It's like sitting through a really bad movie. If you don't stick it out until the final scene, you may miss the surprise ending that was better than anything you've ever seen before.

12
The Conundrum

Johann Anderson was unsure. He hadn't felt so confused and helpless since his own days as an apprentice. He just couldn't figure it all out. He had been on hundreds of Folkteller assignments, maybe even thousands. But the Transit had never acted this way before. What's more, he'd never, ever had to worry about teens from another dimension hitchhiking their way into his study. But his greatest worry came from the new, overaggressive nature of the Shadow People. Before, these creatures had been only haunters—lurking, watching, and hovering over humanity. But now, they were predators—tracking his steps, determining his next movement, as if they were getting ready to pounce and devour their prey at any minute.

On the surface, it seemed like everything was under control. There were only a few weeks left until the Transit would open up again and he could send Wendy back to her own world. But in reality, Aaron's grandfather had never been as uncertain about things as he was at this moment. It was that feeling you have just after a bolt of lightning crackles through the sky down to your own backyard. In that brief moment after the lightning strike, you tense up and brace for that giant clap of thunder. Sometimes, there is no boom, only the silence of the rain. But other times, you shudder and shake with the reverberation of a force that rattles you down to your very bones.

The creaking of the mahogany front door snapped Aaron's grandfather out of his swirling thoughts.

"Pap!" called a familiar voice. "It's me, Aaron! And I've got Jake and Wendy with me!"

That familiar call was such a welcome sound to Johann. It was a call that harkened back to the days when everything was normal and predictable. Lately, it seemed like those days would never return.

For years, Johann Anderson had performed his duties as a Folkteller with delicate precision. Each assignment was completed to the satisfaction of all parties involved, even though there were some bumps along the way. He had kept the Shadow People at bay with his stories, his positive energy, and the occasional never-ending tale. But this latest adventure seemed to draw a great amount of energy out of him—far too much energy. The Shadow People were growing stronger, and there were no guarantees that they would ever get Wendy back to her own world. These were the thoughts that tormented the old Folkteller as the young, bright faces entered his main hallway.

"Ahoy, my boys! And girl!" Pap said in his best grandfatherly voice.

"Hi, Pap!" the troop greeted him in unison as they stepped further into the old house.

"I had almost forgotten that you were coming today. In fact, I've completely forgotten to get your regular refreshments ready. Perhaps you all could help me in the kitchen?"

"Sure, we'd love to," Wendy said with a brightness no one had seen since her arrival.

"Yeah, Pap, just tell us what you need," Jake added.

Aaron watched his two friends in wonderment. He couldn't figure it out. Wendy and Jake never had two words to say to each other. Now, all of the sudden, they were acting like best pals. It was weird, and it made Aaron uncomfortable.

Aaron elbowed Jake in the ribs. "Hey, what gives with you and Wendy?" he whispered.

"Huh? What are you talking about?" Jake whispered back.

"It's just that you guys seem pretty chummy all of the sudden, that's all," Aaron responded in a hushed tone.

"You're nuts," Jake shot back coolly. "Now drop it, will ya?"

"Fine, whatever..." Aaron left the conversation alone for the time being.

Pap led the small party into the kitchen. He directed them to set the farmhouse table with glasses, small plates, and cloth napkins. While they were busy doing that, Pap brought out the root beer and other snacks from the refrigerator and placed them neatly on the table. It always amazed Aaron's grandfather how hungry teenagers could be after one day of school. What seemed like an overabundance of cold cuts, cheese, and crackers was soon reduced to mere tidbits and scraps that would leave a mouse complaining for more.

Pap listened intently as his young friends shared the

stories and tales of their day. He always enjoyed the energy of young people, their voices filling his house, even as they emptied his pantry.

Aaron's attention had moved from his friend and the Wendy girl over to his quiet grandfather. Aaron sensed that something was bothering Pap.

"Pap, you seem really quiet today. Is something bugging you?"

"Now, why would you ask that, boy?" His grandfather did his best to fake it, but Aaron knew better.

"You're never this quiet, Pap, and besides, you haven't even told us a story yet. That's usually the first thing you do."

"You're right, my boy, you're right." Pap thought for a minute and continued, trying to distract his guests from his unusual mood. "Instead of a story this time, how about a riddle?"

"Oh, I love riddles!" Wendy clapped her hands together with excitement. The boys just shrugged their shoulders unfazed, as if to say, "Sure, go ahead."

With that, Pap picked up the familiar old leather book he had surprisingly left on the kitchen counter. He released the clasp and opened up to one of the dog-eared corners, running his finger halfway down the page. He then leaned slowly over the table and put forth the following conundrum:

It creeps along the walls and floors.
It enters rooms through fast, locked doors.
It fills what's empty with subtle black
And fades the day both front and back.
It's here and gone within the night,
Grows only through the shrinking light.

All of the teens sat in deep silence, trying to figure out Pap's riddle. As Johann watched them, he could see them reciting the riddle to themselves, within their heads and partially upon their mumbling lips. Pap smiled a gentle smile, the kind that comes with the satisfaction of making young minds work.

"I've got it!" Wendy shouted after a long silence. "It's darkness!"

"Very close, my dear, but not quite," Pap replied.

"Is it night?" Jake wondered out loud.

"No, but very nearly," Pap chuckled.

"I think I know," Aaron said thoughtfully. "It's death." Pap furrowed his brow at Aaron's answer, as it made him shiver with a sudden chill. "No, boy, it's not that, thank goodness."

The teenagers were stumped. None of the answers they gave were correct. Finally, after dozens of guesses and multiple tries, Aaron conceded for the group. "Okay, we give up—what's the answer?"

"*It's shadow*," Pap said in a tone that was both calm

and foreboding, like a secret that you wish had remained hidden. This was the riddle that he'd been trying to figure out for himself. He'd never really found the answer, but it hadn't bothered him until the past few days.

Aaron, Jake, and Wendy thought that Pap had known the answer all along. But he had just figured it out himself.

"Isn't shadow the same thing as night or darkness?" Jake asked, like he'd been cheated out of his right answer.

"No, no, not really," Aaron's grandfather answered cautiously. "The dark, night, and blackness are present within time. They are a state of being, making up the cycles of our days. Day turns to night and night turns back into day.

"But a shadow is something quite different. It is the passing from light to dark or dark to light. It's neither day nor night. Shadows are never really present in time; they're in between. They are the manifestation of forces passing through this world: the forces that duck inside the darkness and across the light."

Aaron got the same shiver that Pap had felt when he had figured out the riddle. "Why do I suddenly feel that that everything you're telling us isn't just about this puzzle?"

Pap turned toward his grandson and stated plainly, "Because now we can't wait any longer. Your formal apprentice training needs to begin immediately."

13
A Formal Education

Aaron was beginning to dread weekends. Pap understood the importance of regular school from Monday to Friday, but Saturday and Sunday were now fully dedicated to his young pupil's education.

Aaron arrived every Saturday and Sunday morning at Pap's house, where he'd spend hours and hours reading through volumes of folk and fairy tales. This was not what the teen had expected. He'd envisioned more magical and exciting lessons: ones that included casting spells or flying to far-off lands for battle and adventures. But no such luck—he had been relegated to digging through musty old books filled with stories from all around the world. Those were Pap's orders: *theory before practice.*

It was ten thirty a.m. on a Sunday morning when Aaron had finally had enough. "Pap, this stinks! My eyes hurt, my fingers ache, and I feel like my head is going to explode! I don't want to be an apprentice anymore."

The boy's grandfather grinned a little without displaying his amusement. "Why, what's the problem, Aaron?"

"I'm tired of all of these books. Is this all there is to becoming a Folkteller? I thought I'd get to do what you do—travel across dimensions, fight shadow creatures, and have adventures, you know?"

"Aaron," Pap replied with a deep kindness in his voice, "be careful what you ask for, my boy. For you may certainly get it. All these things will come in their own good time. You have to be a bit more patient and pick up the basics. I mean, how do you expect to become a teller of tales if you have no tales to tell?"

Aaron thought about that for minute. "Yeah, Pap, I understand, but you haven't even let me look at the guidebook yet. If you just let me take a peek, I'm sure that it would help me with my other studies."

The young teen's request gave his grandfather pause, as he pondered if the time was really right to share some of the book's secrets with his eager student. "You make a valid point, Aaron. Let's have a look at the guide, shall we?"

Aaron jumped up from his pile of books and scooted over to where Pap was standing. His grandfather went behind the desk and pulled the ancient Folkteller's Guidebook out from its secret compartment within the drawer. He brought the book over to the leather couch and sat down with Aaron at his side. He then handed the book carefully to his anxious apprentice, along with the key.

Aaron had never really examined the book before. Though it looked really old and worn, it wasn't. The brown leather was soft and smooth. The words on the spine were a little faded, but the gold lettering still showed through, and it was easy to read.

The teen inserted the key and released the stiff clasp, opening the ancient text slowly. The binding creaked a bit, as if it was welcoming him inside a mysterious, hidden room. He read the words on the first page of the guide, and got the shivers just like before, when he'd first seen them—*Stories that won't be read must be told.*

As Aaron leafed through the handwritten pages, he realized something strange. He couldn't understand anything that he was reading. The only things that made any sense to him were the names of the authors, who had inscribed the inner cover of the guide. On that inner cover, he could read some of the names:

Lewis Carroll
Carlo Collodi
Jacob Grimm
Wilhelm Grimm
Charles Perrault
Mark Twain
Alexander Pushkin
Hans Christian Andersen

There were more names, but he couldn't read them because they were written in different foreign languages.

Aaron wondered, "Pap, are these the people who wrote the guide?"

"No, my boy, but they are the ones who've added to it over the years. They've added their own notes throughout the guide, which have proven very helpful to the rest of us. But as far as the original author of this book, well, no one really knows. All of the Folkteller Guidebooks are derived from the first one that was ever written, so many years ago."

Aaron was even more intrigued with the book now. As he turned more pages and went deeper into the guide, a strange thing happened. With each turn of the page, the words would fade in and out like a blinking television screen that was about to lose its picture. The words themselves pulsed and began to morph into odd letters and symbols. Now even the English words and letters that he could read before became completely illegible.

The teen grabbed his grandfather's arm and pointed to the pages that were transforming before his eyes. "Pap, look! What's happening?!"

Johann Anderson took the book from his nervous grandson. "Not to worry, my boy. You've done nothing wrong. It's just the book telling you that you're done for now. You've seen all you need to see."

"I don't understand," Aaron said with a look of discouragement and confusion.

"Aaron, the guidebook is for Folktellers only. It provides us with the information we need, when we need it—not just when we want it. It's to be used to as a tool that fosters our mission, not as a weapon that fosters our own selfish desires and interests. The book was just responding to your desire to know more. It was protecting you from your own human weakness. It was protecting you from yourself. Remember, you're not a true Folkteller yet. You're still an apprentice."

What Pap said weighed heavy on Aaron's mind and heart. He couldn't help but feel that there was so much more to learn. Maybe he wasn't cut out to be a Folkteller after all? This seemed like a lot of work, and there weren't any guarantees that he'd ever finish his studies.

Just as his thoughts began to weigh heavy on his mind, there was a knock on Pap's front door. Aaron's gloomy spell was broken for a moment as he jumped up and ran out of the library. When he opened the old door, he was pleasantly surprised to see Jake and Wendy standing there with a bag of fast food and soft drinks.

"We thought we'd come kidnap you!" Wendy said with a voice of optimistic energy.

"Yeah, it's time to take a break!" Jake added.

It's amazing what one little act of kindness can do. Just seconds ago, Aaron had been wallowing in his own gloom. Now, as if by magic, his friends showed up and were ready to turn his mood around.

"Wow, thanks, guys! You don't know how glad I am to see you." Aaron smiled and exhaled as he welcomed his friends back into the library.

"So, this is what you've been doing with your weekends?" Jake asked as he looked around the room. There were books, papers, pencils, pens, and handwritten notes strewn about the place.

"It is kind of a mess," Wendy said quietly, "But it looks like you've been thumping the thornpick too hard."

"What?" Aaron answered. "I have no idea what you just said, Wendy."

"Sorry," Wendy explained. "Where I come from, that means you've been working a lot, and maybe it's time for a break."

Aaron pushed back some of the books and papers to make room for his french fries and Coke. "It's been pretty crazy, trying to keep up with all of my schoolwork, along with this stuff."

As Aaron opened up his fast food bag, Wendy began leafing through the notes and papers that lay all around them. In a pile of books, she noticed one that looked very familiar to her.

"Is that Pap's guidebook?" she said with slight surprise.

"Yup," Aaron gulped between mouthfuls of hamburger and french fries.

"I'm surprised that he'd let you even touch it," Jake said.

"Yeah, that's a pretty special book to leave just lying on the floor," Wendy added.

"Not as much as you'd think," Aaron answered curtly. "Go ahead; open it up if you want to."

Wendy and Jake looked a little puzzled and hesitated.

"Go ahead," Aaron urged them with a sly grin. "It's okay—I am a Folkteller-in-Training, after all."

109

Jake took the book first. He opened up the creaky leather cover and began slowly flipping through the pages. There was a little bit of handwriting on the inside cover, like he'd seen before when Pap showed them the book. But as he flipped through the pages, an odd look came over his face. He started to flip faster, moving his fingers back and forth in between the pages as if he was looking for something he'd lost.

"Hey, there's nothing on these pages—they're all blank," Jake said with a puzzled stare.

Aaron chuckled out loud. "Are you sure? That book wasn't blank when I read it. It's full of stuff!"

"Nuh-uh, look!" Jake held open the book to show Aaron and Wendy the empty pages.

"Oh, that's right; I forgot to tell you—that book's for Folktellers only!"

"So, it's enchanted?" Wendy asked in wonder.

"Um, I guess so," Aaron answered with disinterest.

"May I see the book?" Wendy asked Jake politely.

"Sure, take it."

Jake handed Wendy the book and she began to leaf through the pages.

"Well, nothing, right?" Jake questioned.

Wendy hesitated a little, as if she was looking at something that she didn't want the others to know. She seemed to be stalling as her eyes clung to a single page in the book. "Y-yes... I don't see anything on these pages. Each one I look at is totally blank, just like Jake said."

It was the tone in Wendy's voice that made Jake and Aaron question whether Wendy was really looking at blank pages in the book.

"Are you sure that you don't see *anything*?" Aaron inquired.

"Nope, not a thing!" Wendy said quickly as she slammed the book shut.

"Wendy, be careful!" Aaron shouted as he gently took the book from her, coddling it with great care. "That book is not only powerful; it's sacred to us Folktellers!"

Aaron regretted having used such a precious object to play a trick on his friends.

Wendy replied nervously, "W-Well, I'm not a Folkteller, so I didn't know, sorry! Besides, I couldn't see anything anyway."

"It's okay." Aaron calmed down. "There's no way you could know, or even see anything. Pap said the book is protected from anyone who isn't a Folkteller."

"What's that supposed to mean?" Jake shot back with a look of disbelief.

"It *means* that you can only see what you're supposed to see—nothing more and nothing less. That's why you guys didn't see anything."

"Makes sense to me," Wendy said, as if she was holding something back.

"Whatever," Jake replied dismissively. "Who cares, anyway… It's just one less thing that I've got to worry about."

The room was uncomfortably quiet for a few minutes. There was a feeling between friends that some things were not being shared. Nobody brought it up specifically, but you could feel the tension in the room, like an overtightened guitar string. It was as if they were all were waiting for the string to snap and the guitar to twang loudly. Then they could all jump up together in singular surprise.

But the string never snapped and the twang never came. The tension remained until Aaron quietly picked up the Folktellers Guidebook and placed it carefully back into his grandfather's desk drawer.

14
The Compendium of Extraordinary Things

"You're ready for this now." Pap removed a thick, heavy volume from his library shelf and handed it down to Aaron.

"What is it?" Aaron asked, as if he dreaded being handed another book.

"It's the next phase in your training, and a very important one at that," Pap replied.

"Can't I just go on a mission with you?" Aaron begged. "I'd learn so much more that way."

Pap reminded his grandson, "Remember, theory before practice. You'll thank me later for this, I promise."

The cover had been crafted in ancient black leather, decorated with silver filigree and ornate Tellerian symbols. Tellerians were the people who came from the ancient, folktelling traditions. These were their signs, used by Folktellers throughout the ages.

The book read, *Compendium of Extraordinary Things*, with no author credit.

The giant binding creaked as Aaron opened the massive tome. His eyes widened as the first words flowed into his brain and heart, like a spirit possessing his soul:

Welcome to the *Folkteller Universe.*

This is a place spun up from the dust of stories shared, and this book is but a single gathering of that collected cosmic dust.

Before you enter this universe, I feel compelled to warn you—a book is a powerful thing. And this one is no exception.

It is neither good nor evil, but has the capacity for both. The catalyst, of course, is you.

And therein lies the adventure... and the danger.

Aaron was completely captivated by these words. This was the book he had been waiting for. It was filled with things beyond his imagination, answering numerous questions that had been piling up in his head.

This was the book that explained in detail how the Folktellers came to be. It provided a catalog of mythological creatures and monsters that grew out of folklore and legend—including the Shadow People. It even included some basic rules of the Folkteller Universe.

Hours passed, but they seemed like minutes. The teen's brain was swimming. So much to learn, so much information. It was almost too much to handle. Half of the stuff he didn't even understand, but he couldn't help but be entranced by what the pages revealed.

Aaron finally lifted his head out of the massive book. The light was just starting to turn purple outside.

"Almost six o'clock already...," Aaron mumbled to himself as he got up off the floor, where he had been reading. Pap had left him alone hours ago, vacating the library for another part of the house.

He closed the heavy cover and laid the book on the edge of Pap's desk. Before he left the library, Aaron turned around once, shook his still-swimming head, and wondered, "What have I gotten myself into?"

As the teen turned the corner into the hallway, he was completely unaware of the shadows that sifted silently into the empty library.

15
The Secret Couple

Jake sat right next to Wendy on the park bench. They had been seeing a lot of each other ever since Aaron began his formal apprentice training. They weren't officially boyfriend and girlfriend. But it was clear that they really liked each other.

Jake reached down to his side and fumbled for Wendy's hand, hidden on the bench seat between them. Wendy weaved her fingers in between Jake's fingers, and felt his slightly sweaty palm as their hands clasped together.

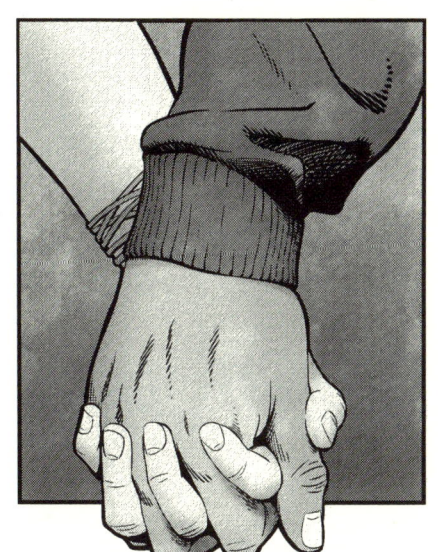

Jake couldn't bring himself to look Wendy directly in the eyes. Instead he stared straight ahead, focusing on the jungle gym and the set of swings that rose and fell before him. As he watched the little kids playing and going back and forth on the swings, he could feel his heart doing the same. There was something about Wendy that gave him the same feeling—the excitement of soaring to the highest heights and the queasiness of being pulled back to reality—all in a single motion.

Wendy turned to Jake. "You know, it's going to be a full moon next week." The words burned in Jake's ears. He knew that Wendy would have to go back to her world soon, but he worked hard to forget that fact. It was something he just didn't want to deal with, so he didn't.

"Did you hear what I said?" she asked.

"Uh, yeah, I heard you." Jake's voice cracked.

"That means I'll have to go back soon," Wendy reminded him.

"Uh-huh...," Jake replied, afraid that he might lose control of his tears.

"So, what do you think...about us?" Wendy wondered softly.

Jake turned toward Wendy. He didn't care any more about crying, or yelling and losing it altogether. He just knew that he had to say something. "Wendy, I really like you."

Wendy smiled, "I really like you, too."

"Well, can't you just stay here?" Jake asked hopefully.

Wendy pursed her lips softly and tried to hold back her own tears. "I'd really like to, Jake, but my family…my friends…everything…it's back there."

"I'm not," Jake stated firmly.

"No, you're not," Wendy said sincerely, "but you're here with me now. Maybe that's all that matters. We have today, so why can't we just enjoy it, you know—together?"

Jake pulled his hand away from Wendy and folded his arms across his chest. "Maybe it's just easier to cut things off now. Why should we be together when we know it's gonna end anyway?"

Wendy nodded slowly. "Maybe you're right, Jake. That would be easier. We could just spend the next week not talking to each other and avoiding eye contact. Sure, we'd be uncomfortable and awkward around each other, but that would make it easier when I go back—easier for both of us. Is that what you want?"

Jake looked back out at the playground. He watched the little kids run around and hang from the jungle gym. He could hear them yelling and squealing with shouts of joy. Their shouts seemed to be a language all of their own. Then an odd thing happened. He fully expected to become overwhelmed with anger, frustration, and depression. But he didn't. Instead, Jake was overcome by a feeling of beautiful sadness. It was the kind of sadness that comes when you feel yourself completely present within the inevitable passing of time. You aren't dwelling on the past or looking deep into the future. You are in the moment, surrounded by the warmth and love of someone who genuinely cares about you. It was like slipping into a warm bath, where your body tingles, relaxes, and succumbs to the soft weight of the water.

"Is that what you want?" Wendy repeated.

Jake looked back at Wendy and simply said, "No."

"Well, what do you want?" Wendy asked plainly.

"It's not what I want. I can't have what I want," Jake thought out loud. "It's about dealing with what I've got."

"So, what *have* you got?" Wendy asked curiously.

"I have you for another week. And it's gonna be the best week of my life."

Wendy smiled warmly. Jake took her hand in his once again. Together, they looked out over the park and watched as the children continued their play, both wishing this moment could last forever.

16
Progress

Pap was frustrated. He busied himself with straightening up the books in his library, handling the editions with pursed lips and a furrowed brow.

Despite his best efforts, it seemed that Aaron wasn't learning a darn thing. The teen had spent weekend after weekend over at Pap's house, listening to stories, reading through old books, and working with his grandfather on the tone and quality of his storytelling voice. But everything felt flat and lifeless.

Pap leaned back in his leather desk chair. "What's the problem, Aaron? You don't seem to care about what we're doing here."

Aaron looked up from his seat on the couch. "I don't know Pap—I guess my heart hasn't really been in this stuff lately."

Pap studied his grandson's expression. He saw the worry lines cut deeper into Aaron's face. Perhaps he was asking too much of the young man. He was too young for worry lines.

"You doin' all right, Aaron?" Pap asked.

Aaron didn't answer right away. He was too deep in his own thoughts, trying to sort out the pages, images, and feelings that swirled back and forth through his jostled brain. His head felt like a deck of new cards that had been poorly shuffled by a pair of clumsy hands. His thoughts flipped over each other until an odd idea caused the entire deck to explode out to the edges of his skull.

Eventually, Aaron sorted his loose thoughts and responded to his grandfather's question. "It's not too much, Pap. It's just that I don't know that I'll ever be any good at it. How can I ever help people discover the truth about themselves?"

"What makes you ask that?" Pap asked in earnest.

"Well," Aaron began, "it's like the story of one of the Roman gods, who in a moment of joy decided to make humankind a present."

Without realizing it, Aaron's voice began to change. As if in a trance, Aaron began to tell a story in a resonant tone that didn't seem like his own:

He sent his messenger down to earth to tell the world, "Mortals, the great Jupiter has opened for your benefit his all-gracious hands. It is true he made you somewhat

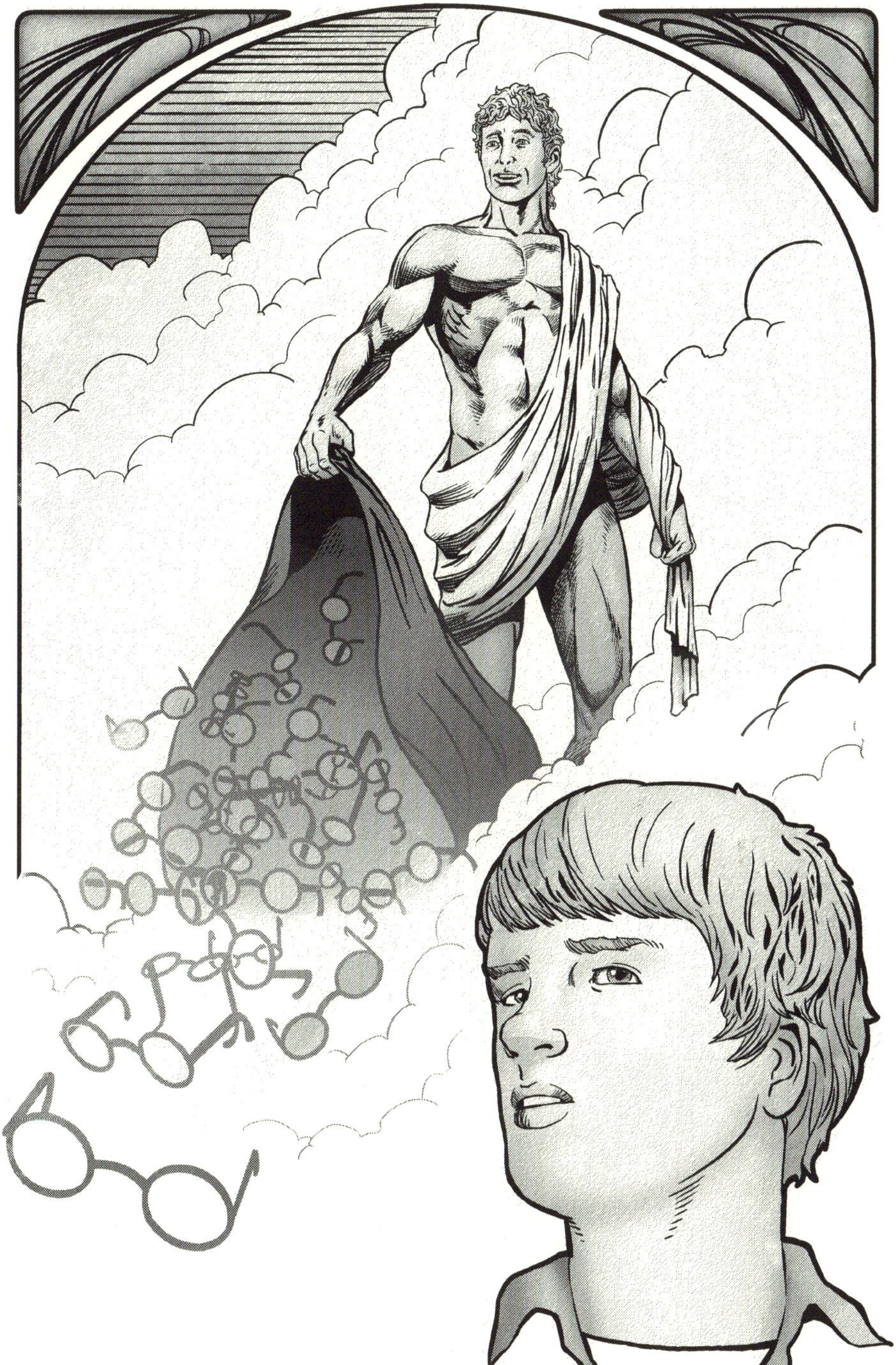

shortsighted, but to remedy that inconvenience, behold how he has favored you!"

So saying, the messenger unloosed his bag, and an infinite number of spectacles tumbled out. All of the humans picked them up with great eagerness. There was enough for everyone, and each person got a pair. But it was soon found that these spectacles didn't make all objects appear the same to humanity, for one pair was purple, another blue; one was white and another black. Some of the other glasses were red, some green, and some yellow. There were more colors than one could count. The funny thing was that every person was charmed by their own pair of spectacles, believing in their hearts that their pair was the best. And in doing so, humanity enjoyed the firm opinion that their perspective through each pair of glasses was the one and only truth. And as it was then, so it is today.

As Aaron finished his story, the trance he was under seemed to fade. His eyes focused back into the center of the room and he fell silent again.

Pap stood up and clapped his hands together heartily. He was very pleased.

"Well done, my boy, well done!"

"Wh-what are you talking about, Pap?" Aaron was still a bit dazed and had no idea what his grandfather was so excited about.

"You've done it, Aaron—your first storytelling!"

"No, no—it wasn't," Aaron argued. "I was just answering your question, that's all."

Pap cupped Aaron's head in the palms of his hands. "That's what we do, my boy—we answer others' questions through the stories we tell. You are a Folkteller."

Aaron sat back down on the couch. He couldn't believe it—Pap was right. The story he'd just told…he had actually recited one of Aesop's fables from memory. It had just come to him; he didn't even have to think about it. It was just there.

Aesop was an ancient Folkteller that Aaron had been studying ever since his training began. Aesop was credited with a number of fables and stories, including ones that clearly happened long after his time. In fact, no one was really sure if he'd ever existed. But none of that mattered now.

It was amazing that such a young apprentice could remember all of the details of one of his stories after such a short time of study.

Pap continued, "Aaron, the answer you gave me came in the form of a story. Not only did you answer my question, but you also isolated the challenge that all Folktellers have. People see the world as they want to see it, through their own colored glasses. Our job is to change their lenses a little, so that they might discover a new way to look at things. That's how they find the truth!"

The teen hung his head between his knees. "Oh, Pap,

I don't know what the heck I'm doing. If I did anything right just now, it was dumb luck. I'm completely clueless…"

Aaron's grandfather sat down right next to his grandson and put his arm around the boy's slumped shoulders. "Aaron, you are not clueless. In fact, you're one of the most clue-filled young men I've ever met. I know it's hard when you start to come into your own, when you start to realize your true potential. That's what's happening to you right now. It's scary because you feel like things are coming at you a mile a minute. You're either dodging the bullets or trying to catch them in your teeth."

Johann Anderson elbowed his grandson gently in the ribs, drawing a little smile out of the corners of Aaron's mouth. "Sometimes, you have to let things happen, boy. You prepare and study and worry and fret, which is all necessary. But when the moment comes, you have to let it come and be in that moment. That's what you did just now, and it was beautiful."

Aaron's smile was even bigger now, and his head had lifted off of his knees and now rested firmly on his shoulders.

"You really think it was beautiful, Pap?"

"Indeed, it was," Pap answered firmly. "And I think there'll be more to come from you. I really do."

"How can you be so sure?" Aaron said with shadows of doubt in his voice.

"Oh, that's easy," Pap replied, his eyebrows raised with the knowledge of experience. "Once those bullets start flying, you won't have a choice."

17
Abnormal

It was so nice to have a long weekend without any studying. For the first time in what seemed like forever, Aaron was able to stay at home and chill. His grandfather had given him a break from his apprentice training, and Friday was an off day for teacher conferences.

129

Aaron's brother, Marty, came thumping into the kitchen for breakfast.

"Hey, dingus, long time no see!" Marty stated as he knuckle-rubbed his little brother on the top of the head.

"Cut it out, Marty!" Aaron yelled as he ducked his head away from Marty's grinding knuckles.

"Relax, spaz, I'm just joking around. Whadya gonna do, beat me up with one of your powerful stories?"

Aaron shot back, "No, but I might beat you in the head with one of my books!"

Marty snorted a "yeah, right" under his breath and grabbed a box of cereal, a bowl, and some milk from the refrigerator. He then bumbled out of the room, but not before he got one final kick on the back of Aaron's chair.

Aaron swatted at his passing brother but decided not to chase him. He wondered if Marty was jealous that Aaron had been chosen as a Folkteller's apprentice instead of him. Marty was the older brother, so it would have made more sense for him to be the one. But Pap had said it wasn't a personal choice—the universe picks who it picks, that's it.

A big part of Aaron *wanted* Marty to be the one. He was stronger and better suited to be the hero—better than Aaron, anyway.

In a weird way, Aaron was happy his brother was teasing him. At least it was a pain he knew. He knew that Marty could be cruel, but he was used to it.

Things had been so crazy lately that Aaron craved all the regular things he used to do. Suddenly, all the ordinary, everyday stuff seemed really important. For the past week, Aaron had actually liked getting up in the morning for school, going to classes, coming home and having dinner with his family, and just being normal.

Now he had an extra day to just be a regular kid, and he was going to enjoy it. He had invited Jake and Wendy to watch some movies this afternoon. It seemed like ages since they had had any time to talk. He didn't even care anymore if Jake and Wendy were dating. Aaron was just glad to have them around. Besides, Wendy was going back in a few days, so none of that really mattered.

The knock at the side door made Aaron jump. He knew his friends were coming over, but he hadn't expected them so soon. He ran into the side hall and opened the door for his welcome guests.

"Hey, bud, great to see you!" Jake greeted his friend with a wide smile and a pat on the back.

"Hi, Aaron," Wendy said sweetly from behind her unofficial boyfriend.

"Hey, guys, come on in!" Aaron brought his friends through the kitchen and into the family room. He had spent the past half hour getting the room ready with drinks, snacks, and the couch cushions positioned for optimal comfort.

It was a cold, cloudy afternoon, and the dull sky

threatened rain without ever following through. But inside, the soft light of the family room warmed the mood. The three friends were curled up on the couch like a litter of puppies in a blanket-filled basket, watching the movie flicker across the glowing television screen.

It was right at that moment, when the world completely faded away and Aaron's body finally relaxed, that the mood changed remarkably.

The once dull, gray sky now swirled around itself, like a bowl of murky soup being ladled across the horizon. Jake, Wendy, and Aaron felt the room go cold.

It was the Shadow People, Aaron could sense it. He knew they wanted something, but he didn't know what. They were coming closer and closer, seeping into his once-warm room.

In one way, he was sad and afraid. In that moment before all hell broke loose, Aaron knew that things would never be like they used to be, never as comfortable and safe. But in another way, he felt stronger. He could feel the courage rising up from his chest and flowing throughout the rest of his body.

For better or worse, this was going to be his new normal.

"What the heck is happening?!" Jake yelled to no one in particular. His body was plastered up against the couch cushions and he couldn't move.

Wendy tried to pry herself up off the couch, but to

no avail. She was stuck worse than Jake and couldn't move a muscle.

It was Aaron they had come for. The funny thing was that Aaron was the only one who wasn't held down by the shadowy force. It was as if they were challenging him. It was as if they wanted to test his powers to see how strong he really was.

"What do you want?!" Aaron shouted into the air with his fists clenched and his arms extended, ready for a fight.

But no answer came.

Aaron whipped around to face the shadowy wisps that held his friends so tightly. "I'm ordering you to let them go!" he pronounced with authority and defiance.

Still no reply.

"What are you waiting for?" Aaron's question hovered above the room, anticipating some sort of answer.

And then the answer came. It came soft and slow, like a faint echo rising out of a desolate canyon. "Flesh…give…us…book…"

The rasp and wheeze of these words scratched at their eardrums. Wendy, Jake, and Aaron would have covered their ears if they could have, but it was too late. Those four words slid across their brains, like a dead body being dragged down a long hallway.

"Flesh…give…us…book…," they heard again, with excruciating clarity this time.

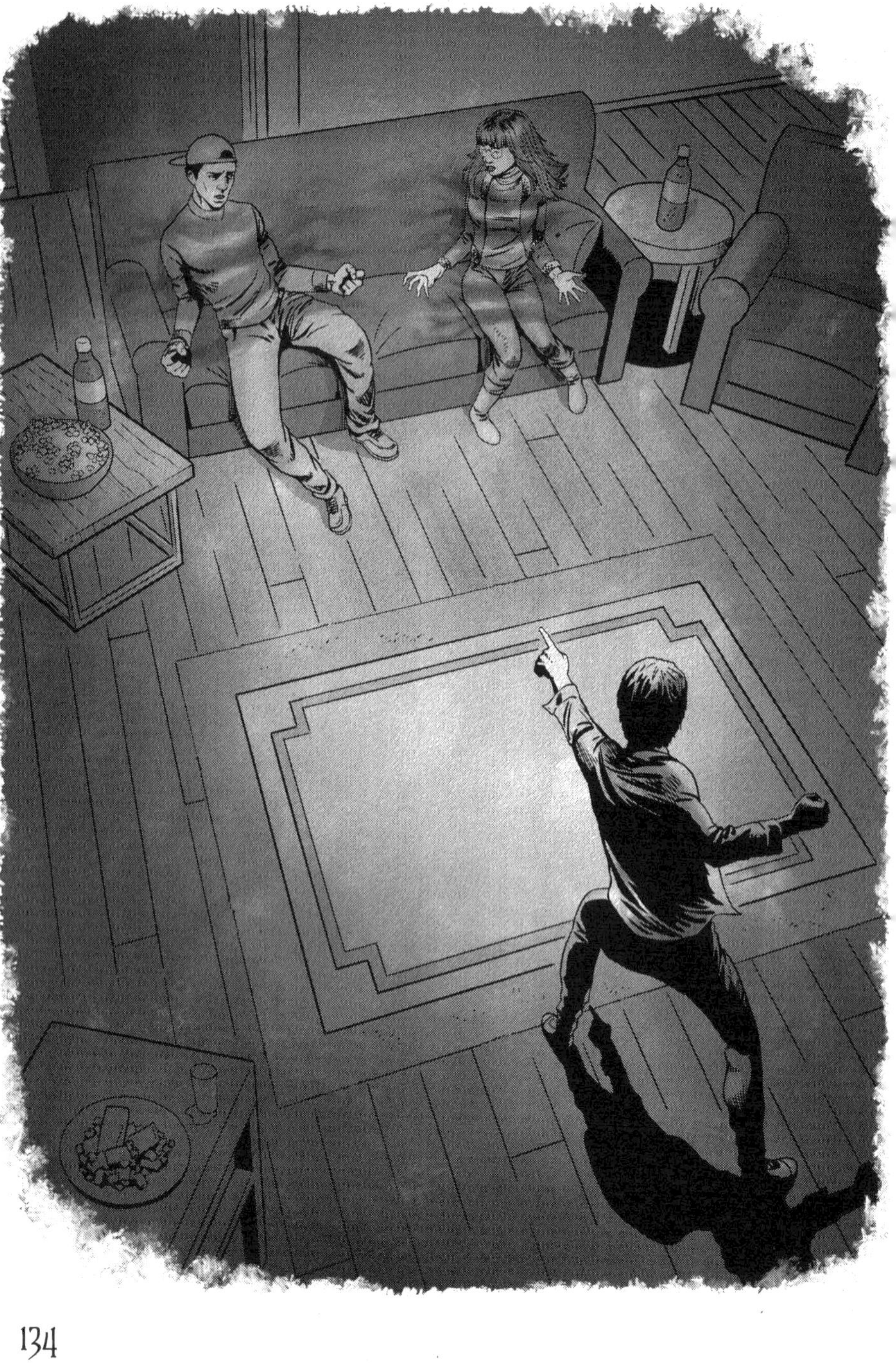

"I don't have it." Aaron strained to hide his pain and confusion at their awful refrain.

"Flesh is liar...," their voices rang, as if an ancient bell were tolling the one o'clock hour.

"He's not lying!" Wendy shot back. "He doesn't have it!"

"Yeah, it's not even his!" Jake added. "It's his pap's!"

Aaron looked over at Jake, still stuck in the creases of the couch. He gave him a look that he should shut his mouth right away. Jake was very familiar with that look and suddenly became very quiet. Aaron glanced over at Wendy and told her to keep quiet too, without saying a word. Wendy knew exactly what Aaron meant and fell silent immediately.

For the next few minutes, an eerie silence filled the family room. The Shadow People were still there. They hardly moved. Instead they seemed to float all in one place, as if they were waiting for the teens to make the next move. But Jake, Wendy, and Aaron knew better. They now knew that these creatures were responding to their every movement, to their every word. On sheer instinct, they decided to remain quiet and still. They would let the Shadow People do something first.

Time seemed to stand still in those waiting moments. It seemed like seconds were days and minutes were years as the teens refrained from any movement or speech.

Then suddenly, there was a sense of release. The Shadow People let go of Wendy and Jake and gathered together in the middle of the room. The cold that surrounded the teenagers shifted over to where the dark entities were standing. It appeared as if they were holding hands, even though they didn't really have any. The strange creatures began to swirl and spin in a circular motion, like in some bizarre childhood game They spun faster and faster and faster until a black vortex was created in the middle of the room.

Then, in a brief but powerful flash of black—the shadows were gone.

18
Knowledge Is Power

Nobody could move. Despite the fact that the creatures were gone, Wendy and Jake remained frozen on the couch. Wendy gently shook her arms and legs like she was trying to reawaken her sleeping limbs. Aaron would have had no trouble moving if he'd wanted to, but he stood in place instead. He was trying to process everything that had just happened. His brain hadn't caught up with reality yet.

"Aaron, are you okay?" Wendy asked quietly.

"I'm fine," Aaron answered softly with a little rasp in his voice.

"Those things were seriously messed up," Jake declared, having a tough time explaining what had just happened.

"Uh-huh," Aaron responded, still deep in thought, but angry. "They really crossed the line this time."

"Why do you think they wanted the book so badly?" Wendy wondered out loud.

Jake just shrugged his shoulders. He didn't have a clue. Wendy didn't make a sound but shrugged her shoulders back at Jake. She didn't have a clue either.

They both waited for Aaron to say something. Aaron's brow was furrowed as he continued sorting out the events of the past few minutes in his head.

"I'm glad you're okay, both of you," Aaron said. "It could have been a lot worse. They could have killed us if they wanted to."

"Well, aren't you just a ray of sunshine!" Jake joked.

Wendy didn't think it was very funny and maintained a serious, worried look on her face. "What do you mean, Aaron?"

Aaron spoke more clearly now. "They're a lot more powerful than I thought they were. Pap may not even know how powerful they've become. They're on the attack. They really want the book. I just can't figure out why they want it so badly, right now. That book's been around for years, for centuries. So why now?"

Wendy took a deep breath and stared directly into Aaron's eyes. "I think I know…," she said ominously.

"What? What is it, Wendy?" Jake asked anxiously.

Wendy broke her stare and threw her gaze upon the ground. She nervously answered, "It's Aaron. They know he's new at all of this. He's a young apprentice. Maybe they think he'd be an easy avenue to get the book. That's why they attacked him, instead of all of us."

There was a brief silence before Aaron spoke up again. "She's right. Pap's getting older, and I'm not experienced enough. I think they think we're vulnerable now—at least for a little while."

Jake was working through all of this information. The pieces were starting to come together for him, but he still looked confused.

"Guys, I still don't get it. What's the big deal with the book? It's just a bunch of storytelling stuff. Anyway, it's not like you can kill the Shadow People with it."

"You really don't get it, Jake," Aaron said with full frustration in his voice. "You can't kill Shadow People anyway—they're not living or dead."

"What? That's nuts!" Jake shot back, "They've got to be one or the other."

"Not necessarily," Wendy added thoughtfully.

"They may be in that place between life and death… Remember, Pap said they might be remnants of lost souls who never listened to their own stories."

"The book controls them," Aaron stated matter-of-factly. "It's the one thing that holds them back. The stories push back the darkness."

"So what do you think they'd do with the book if they got their hands on it?" Jake asked point-blank.

Aaron thought about Jake's question for a minute and answered, "It's less about them doing anything with the book. It's more about us not having it."

"Oh, I get it," Wendy continued. "They want to take our weapon away; without it, we'd be powerless against them."

"Something like that," Aaron acknowledged. "But the book is more than just a weapon to use on enemies. In fact, you can't use it that way anyway. Pap taught me that the Folkteller's Guidebook is a gathering of knowledge. Its power is based upon the Folktellers of the past, present, and future. It's the physical collection of all that we've learned over the centuries… To lose it would mean to lose our history, maybe even ourselves."

"So, what if they got it?" Jake pushed the issue. "What would happen then?"

"I don't know—maybe they'd destroy it," Aaron responded. "All I know is that I don't want to find out.

They're stronger than I thought, and it's clear that we can't handle them ourselves."

"We've got to let Pap know what's going on," Wendy said. "Maybe he'll know what to do."

Jake and Aaron nodded in agreement. Even if Pap had no idea what to do, it just seemed safer at his house. Besides, there was strength in numbers, and one more person on their side was better than standing alone—especially if that person was an experienced, battle-tested Folkteller.

19
That Sick Feeling

On their way over to Aaron's grandfather's house, a strange and horrible thought came over each of the teenagers.

What if the Shadow People were already at Pap's?

Jake said it first, but Aaron and Wendy had already been thinking the same thing.

They'd just kept their mouths shut, figuring that everyone had been spooked enough already.

"What if the Shadow People are at Pap's? They want the book and they know Pap's got it. What if we're too late?!"

"It's never too late to fight," Aaron scolded his friend. "We just have to be ready for anything. Besides, Pap can handle himself with those creeps—he's been doing it for years."

The teens quickened their pace with the notion that Pap might be in trouble. Their brisk walk slowly transformed into a jog and then into a full-on sprint as they rounded the corner near Pap's house.

The front door wasn't locked, as if the old man had been expecting them. Aaron burst through the door with his friends and instinctively yelled, "Pap, it's me!"

From the library came the warm and familiar response: "Ahoy, my boy! I'm in here."

Jake, Wendy, and Aaron scooted quickly down the hallway into the library. They were all looking for confirmation that Pap was all right. As they entered the room, Aaron was mentally prepared to fight the Shadow People. He half expected his grandfather to be tied up in the corner, with one of the dark entities mimicking his voice to draw them in.

But that wasn't the case at all. Everything seemed strangely normal. Pap was sitting on the leather sofa, with his legs stretched out in front of him, quietly reading a book.

"Are you okay?" Aaron asked anxiously.

All three teenagers waited impatiently for his response.

"I'm fine," Pap assured them. "And why wouldn't I be?"

"We just thought they may be after you!" Jake felt the words jump off of his tongue and out of his mouth.

Johann Anderson lowered his book from his face and slid his reading glasses down toward the tip of his nose. "Now, *who* might they be and *why* would they be after *me*?"

Wendy piped up, "Pap, we were just attacked by the Shadow People—at Aaron's house! They thought he had the guidebook—they wanted to take it from him!"

Pap rested his book on his lap and began to stroke his chin with his right hand. "Well, that's quite a story—and a strange one at that."

"Why do you think it's strange, Pap?" Aaron wondered. "It's not the first time we've had a run-in with those demons."

"No—no, I don't find the attack so strange, though I am most certainly concerned for your safety and happy that no one was hurt. No, it's rather this book I've been reading for the past few hours or so. It's just so odd that I should be drawn to it, today of all days."

"What is it?" Jake asked. "Is it the guidebook?"

"No, it's not," Aaron's grandfather answered. "In fact, it's a book of poetry—by T. S. Eliot. I've been reading and re-reading this one poem for hours. It's called *The Hollow Men*, and its stanzas were echoing in my head right up until I heard all of you bluster through my front door."

At that moment, Pap picked up his book again and began to read the foreboding poem:

Between the idea
And the reality
Between the motion
And the act
Falls the Shadow
For Thine is the Kingdom

Between the conception
And the creation
Between the emotion
And the response
Falls the Shadow
Life is very long

Between the desire
And the spasm
Between the potency
And the existence

Between the essence
And the descent
Falls the Shadow
For Thine is the Kingdom

For Thine is
Life is
For Thine is the

This is the way the world ends
This is the way the world ends
This is the way the world ends
Not with a bang but a whimper.

There was silence as Pap's words circled slowly about the room like the gray smoke of a fresh-snuffed candle.

"Well, that's kind of depressing," Wendy said flatly.

"What's it mean?" Jake seemed confused again.

Aaron wasn't quite sure what it all meant, but he had a hunch. It was weird that Pap was obsessing over that poem right at the time when he and his friends were being attacked. There had to be a connection.

While Aaron wrestled with his thoughts, his grandfather endeavored to answer Jake's question: "This poem, this bit of verse that has been weaved into my thoughts, is a warning. A message of some sort."

"Who sent it?" Wendy asked with even greater intrigue.

"The question is not *who* sent it," Johann Anderson stated thoughtfully; "it's more about *why* it was sent. The poem was warning me about your attack and the renewed interest in the guidebook by the Shadow People."

"What do you mean by the 'renewed interest' of the Shadow People? Have they come after the book before?" Pap's words had rattled Aaron out of his own thoughts.

"My boy, they've been after that book for millennia. They've never stopped trying to get their blackened claws on our sacred tome."

Aaron was upset. "Pap, why didn't you tell me about this before? You knew and didn't say a word! We were almost killed!"

Johann Anderson set his book down and stood up with such strength and purpose that the teens all took a few steps back. They looked like scared puppies sliding back on their bottoms in fear of their master's scolding.

Pap's frustration with his grandson finally came to a head. Out of nowhere he yelled, "Uncalled for!" Aaron's grandfather shouted with a clarity and firmness that Aaron had never heard before. "You question my intent, boy? After all I've done for you, all the time I've invested in your future? In your friends?"

Aaron felt horrible. He knew that Pap was his best friend and his greatest protector. He should have trusted him more.

After a moment of awkward silence, Aaron spoke. "I'm sorry, Pap. That was way out of line. I know you'd never let anything bad happen to us on purpose."

"Well, of course not," Pap said comfortingly. "Now let's do a little more sorting out of this situation."

The elder Folkteller walked over to his desk and began shuffling through papers and flipping through a few books he had lying there.

"This is quite unexpected, but in hindsight, I guess I shouldn't be surprised at all," Pap muttered to himself.

"Why shouldn't you be surprised?" Wendy stepped forward toward the desk.

Pap looked up from his papers as if he had been interrupted from sifting through his jumbled thoughts. "W-what did you say?" he stuttered.

"I asked you why you shouldn't be surprised by what the Shadow People did," Wendy repeated.

"Oh, well, that's quite simple, my dear. You see, the Transit will reopen in a few days. The Shadow People are always more active then. They know that we Folktellers are always more vulnerable when we travel interdimensionally. If they're after the book, that would be the best time to attack."

The teens had completely forgotten that the full moon was almost here. Wendy was returning home to her own world in two days. They had been so caught up in their own troubles that they'd never realized how short their time together really was.

Wendy took a deep breath and shuddered. She wanted to go home so badly, but she was going to miss her friends—especially Jake.

Pap continued, "I certainly never expected them to make their move before the onset of the full moon. And the fact that they attacked you young people, well, that's the most reckless thing I've ever seen them do."

"We thought it was because Aaron was so inexperienced. Maybe they thought they could get the upper hand on a rookie," Jake proposed.

"You may have something there, Jake," Pap concurred. "Aaron is a star pupil, to be sure, but there are many things he still needs to learn."

"You know, I love it when people talk about me like I'm not even in the room," Aaron complained.

Pap patted Aaron on the shoulder. "Come now, boy, no need to be so thin-skinned. We're all on the same side, remember?"

"I remember, I remember," Aaron said, slightly exasperated. "What I want to know is what we're going to do about the Shadow People. The Transit will be open on Saturday, and they're sure to be there to cause trouble. I'm a rookie Folkteller, so what?"

It was this plain and simple question that gave everyone a sick feeling in their stomachs. Like a late spring tornado that had been forecasted the night before, Johann Anderson and his teenage friends knew what was coming—yet they really didn't know if it all would end with a bang or a whimper. Nobody felt very good about either option.

20
When One Door Opens

Wendy and Jake were finally alone. They left Aaron's grandfather's house together, while Aaron stayed behind to get some more coaching from Pap. They crossed the long, oak-lined street and made their way through the park.

It was a familiar scene for both Wendy and Jake. They had agreed weeks ago that they wouldn't dwell on her having to go back home. But now that their time together was fading, Jake couldn't help himself.

"Are—are you sure you still wanna go back?"

"Of course, I am—why wouldn't I be?" Wendy snapped.

"I just thought that maybe you'd change your mind, that's all," Jake said quietly.

"If I'd changed my mind, don't you think that you'd have been the first to know?!"

"I'm sorry; I just can't imagine being here without you... I didn't mean to make you mad." Jake scuffed the toe of his shoe against the grass and dirt and shoved his hands into his front pockets.

Wendy started to cry. It started with a slight sniffle in her nose and then a few tears. Before Jake knew what was happening, Wendy had wrapped her arms around his neck and buried her face into his shoulder.

Instinctively, Jake wrapped his arms around her and pulled her close. He could feel the slight convulsions of her body as she took in short breaths between sobs. He touched her hair. That only made her sob more, and he could feel the rapid beat of her heart against his own chest.

Jake was confused. As he held Wendy up, he was sure that if he let her go, she would fall flat on the ground. He had to be strong enough for both of them, even though he felt weak in the knees too. It was the strangest feeling he had ever felt. As badly as he wanted Wendy to stop crying, he hoped against hope that this moment would never end. Jake had never felt so needed, so needy, or so loved as he did right at that moment. It was the fact that Wendy was going away forever that bonded them so close together.

After a time, Wendy's tears began to subside. Sadly, Jake broke the embrace, took Wendy by the shoulders with both hands, and looked straight into her cloudy blue eyes. "Are you gonna be okay?"

"Yeah," Wendy answered calmly, 'I'll be fine. And you?"

Jake didn't answer right away. He took Wendy's hand and they began walking again, which gave him more time to think.

"Wendy, I don't think I'll ever be fine with you having to go back. This past month has been the best month of my life. If I could change things, I would, but I can't. So I guess we'll just have to deal with it, right?" Jake thought that he might start crying too, but he stopped himself. It wasn't that he didn't want Wendy to see him cry. No, he was holding back for the sake of his girlfriend. Jake didn't have to go anywhere; he was staying right where he was in Oakville. Wendy was the one who had to travel through the Transit to get back home. There wasn't any guarantee that she'd even make it back in one piece! No, Jake would keep his emotions in check, for Wendy's sake.

Jake walked Wendy all the way to Aaron's house. They didn't say a word to each other for the rest of the way home. They didn't need to. Each one knew how the other one felt, deep down in their soul—that was enough. What was racing through each of their heads over the next five blocks, only they could tell you.

But one thing was for sure—Jake and Wendy had formed a bond. It was a bond of caring, of selfless love, and of friendship. It was the kind of bond that many people never get to experience in an entire lifetime. Beyond all of this, it was a bond for eternity. For Jake and Wendy knew, without words or promises or contracts, that their love for each other was unbounded by place, time, or the spaces in between.

21
Family

They were just coming up the front path of the house when Aaron's mother came bursting out the front door, shouting, "For the love of all things holy, are you kids all right?" A look of sheer panic was etched on her face. She grabbed Wendy with such force, the girl almost fell backward.

"Mrs. Anderson?" Wendy gasped as the wind was squeezed out of her.

"What gives, Mrs. A?!" Jake demanded, still feeling very protective of Wendy.

"Oh dear, I'm so sorry!" Mrs. Anderson exclaimed. "I just got word about everything that's happened to you kids! Mr. Anderson and I talked to Pap - I just can't believe it!"

"We're fine, we're fine," Wendy assured her as she tried to wriggle out of her loving death grip.

"Yeah, everyone's okay—we're all right," Jake added.

"Well, I had a feeling something like this might happen. I never should have let Pap take Aaron under his wing—oh, I'm a terrible mother!" Mrs. Anderson wailed.

Jake and Wendy looked at each other, not knowing whether to start laughing or to calm Aaron's mom down. It seemed slightly comical to them. The dangerous stuff was all over, and there wasn't any sign of trouble at the Anderson house. But Aaron's mom was still in hysterics.

"Mrs. A, it's not your fault," Jake comforted her. "You did the right thing to let Pap train Aaron. It's his calling. It's what he's supposed to be doing anyway."

This thought had a deep, calming effect on Mrs. Anderson. "I suppose you're right," she said quietly. "All this was inevitable. It would have happened eventually, I guess."

"What's all the commotion out here?" came a voice echoing from the front porch. It was Aaron's dad. He had gotten the news as well, and hadn't realized that Jake and Wendy were there until he heard his wife yelling.

"Hi, Mr. Anderson," Jake said. "We were

just trying to calm Mrs. Anderson down. I guess you guys found out about what happened in your family room?"

"Yes, we did," Mr. Anderson said softly with an air of great seriousness. "When we got home, the house was empty. We thought you were going to be watching movies all afternoon. Well, when we didn't see a note about where you went, we called Pap. He told us everything that had happened and that you two were on your way here."

"Sorry to give you such a scare," Wendy apologized. "We didn't mean to leave without telling anyone. We were just so freaked out, and we knew that Pap would know what to do."

"You did the right thing," Mr. Anderson said. "You should have left us a note or called afterward, but going directly to Pap's house was the right thing to do. The question now is, what do we do about all of this?"

Aaron's mom's eyes got wide, as if some terrible, incredible thought had just filtered into her brain, "Oh my gosh, it's a full moon on Saturday!"

Mr. Anderson pursed his lips. He hadn't forgotten about the full moon, but he hadn't thought that the date was almost upon them. He knew that the Transit would be opening and Wendy had to go home.

Mrs. Anderson reminded him, "Honey, we've got to get Wendy back home!"

"Well, this is a fine time to have all this nonsense happening," Aaron's dad said with an exasperated tone. "You're right: Wendy is our top priority right now—we've got to make sure that she gets back home. This will be our only chance."

"What do you mean 'only chance'?" Jake wondered with a worried look on his face.

"What I mean, Jake, is that the Transit opens every full moon, but it will return someone back home only once. If Wendy misses this lunar cycle, she'll be stranded here forever."

"How do you know?" Jake questioned.

Mr. Anderson put his hand on Jake's shoulder. "Jake, I may not be a Folkteller, but I am a Folkteller's son. Pap taught me a lot too."

Jake looked over at Wendy. One part of him wished that Wendy would miss the opening of the Transit and be stuck in Oakville with him for good. But the other part of him, the part that loved Wendy and put her wants and needs above his own, knew better. He had to do whatever he could to help her get back to her family.

It was right at that moment that Aaron came running up the driveway. "Hey, what's everybody doing out front?"

Aaron's dad responded, "We were just trying to sort things out after your adventure earlier today. Pap said that you were okay—you are, aren't you?"

"Yeah, Dad, I'm fine," Aaron reassured him as he glanced over at his mom and smiled. "Really, I'm okay. I just had to stick around Pap's for a little longer. He had to show me some things before tomorrow."

"What things?" his mother questioned curiously.

"Mom, it's Folkteller stuff. I'm not supposed to talk about it."

Ana Anderson furrowed her brow and frowned. "That seems to be a very popular excuse lately for not telling us things. Secrets can kill, you know. In fact, this whole Folkteller business is more trouble than it's worth!"

"Easy, honey," Jason Anderson said soothingly. "It's not Aaron fault, or Pap's either. They're just doing their jobs. And thank God they are. Just imagine what this world would be like without Folktellers! Why, we'd be overrun by shadows and darkness. I shudder to think what we'd become without someone to share the stories. We've lost three already—let's not let any more go down on our watch."

Mrs. Anderson stepped back a little from the crowd and folded her arms. That was a sign that she understood, and maybe even agreed with her husband. But that didn't mean she was happy about it.

22
Foreshadows

It had been nearly twenty-nine days, twelve hours, forty-four minutes, and three seconds since Wendy arrived in Oakville—one lunar month. Saturday had finally come, and the full moon was scheduled to rise in the late afternoon.

Aaron, Jake, Wendy, and Pap were right. Their instincts had told them that trouble was brewing. Wendy's return to her own dimension would give the Shadow People the opportunity they'd been looking for—the book must be destroyed.

In the shadow realm, the silent shadows gathered. They had tried to steal the book many times before and failed. Three Folktellers were already dead, and still they had nothing to show for it.

But this time was different. The Keeper was much older now. He had lost some of his power, and the one to take his place was still pink and vulnerable—mere Flesh.

So they gathered in their place of emptiness, plotting and scheming without ever saying a word. The old man, the Keeper, was to be their target. They would be unable to defeat him individually, but together they could overcome the old man and retrieve the guidebook.

In their half-floating, shadowy forms, they talked without speech and planned without argument until a decision was made. Without words, they hissed in unison, "The Fetch."

To overtake the Keeper, they would send the Fetch. The Fetch was a unique shadow creature—a wispy, illusive wraith that was able to mimic human form. It was usually sent to retrieve the soul of someone who was about to die. It would appear at night, in the form of the same person they had come to take. It was a doppelganger—a ghostly version of its victim.

The appearance of the Fetch struck fear in all those who saw it, as it was a harbinger of doom and death. The Shadow People controlled the Fetch, and it would do their bidding.

This time, however, its mission would be different. It would be sent as a distraction to Pap in an effort to loosen his grip upon the Folkteller's Guidebook. Of course, the Fetch hoped for something a little more in the bargain. It was sure that if its mission was successful, it would have another soul to carry away for its collection.

At first, it may seem strange that these dark phantasms should be so obsessed with such an old, musty book. It's odd to think that they wanted to possess something without ever using it. No, they sought to gain the book only to destroy it. Their presence in this world would become more powerful because they were able to remove something from it. It's addition by subtraction, and the Shadow People thrived on such dark equations.

This was the diabolical math that Shadow People used for power in this world. They were pure destroyers, whose life force relied on the downfall of others. Fortunately for humanity, there were other forces at play within the earthly realm. Pap, Aaron, Jake, and Wendy were a part of this positive energy. It was the hopeful force that believed in the power of the story and its ability to change the world for the better.

Hopefully, that would be enough to keep the shadows at bay, but there were no guarantees.

23
Waxing and Waning

The face of the moon was almost under the number 15 on the grandfather clock. It was agreed that Jake, Wendy, and Aaron would meet with Pap in his library precisely at three o'clock on Saturday.

The teens were right on time and entered the front door of Pap's house with great trepidation. Aaron opened the heavy mahogany door and yelled cautiously, "Pap, it's me!"

There was a moment of uncomfortable silence. Then they heard Pap yell from the next room, "Ahoy, my boy! Come in and see me!"

That familiar greeting made them all feel better, at least a little bit. As they entered the library, everything seemed almost too normal. Pap was sitting behind his desk, casually leafing through a book as a piping hot cup of tea steamed off to the side.

The teenagers hadn't expected such a quiet, calm scene. In fact, they'd half expected to see Pap tied up and gagged in his leather chair with some sort of sinister, ghostly ropes. They could almost see the Folkteller's Guidebook torn to shreds on the floor by the thick, black claws of the Shadow People.

But they didn't. The scene they came upon in Pap's library was one of an average Saturday—peaceful, calm, and quiet.

Too peaceful, calm, and quiet...

"Hi, Pap!" Wendy said cheerfully as she went around the desk and hugged Aaron's grandfather thickly around the neck. She had never done anything like that before.

"Well, this is quite a surprise!" Pap said, a bit flustered by Wendy's sudden show of affection.

"I thought you were expecting us at three?" Aaron wondered why Pap would be so surprised at their arrival.

"It wasn't your presence that startled me," Pap explained as he straightened his disheveled shirt collar. "It was Wendy's most pleasant greeting and superior arm strength that caused me to wonder—what's gotten into this child?"

"Oh, nothing." Wendy blushed, realizing that she may have been too overzealous with her hug. "I was just glad to see you—uh—to see that everything was all right."

Of course, no one believed her.

Aaron's grandfather saved Wendy from any further awkwardness by changing the subject. "You know, I had the strangest dream last night…"

Jake and Aaron looked over at Pap. They knew he had changed the subject on purpose, but decided not to say anything.

Aaron questioned, "What was it, Pap?"

Pap didn't open his mouth right away. Instead he rubbed his chin thoughtfully, as if he was extracting the thoughts out of his head through his lower jaw.

"It was an early morning dream, the kind that you have after midnight but before the dawn. In fact, I'm still not sure if I was actually asleep… Something disturbed me, and I sat up in bed.—I woke up to a dark room with an odd feeling. It was a feeling like something was standing against the wall, staring at me. But I couldn't see anything, as my eyes hadn't adjusted to the darkness yet.

"Eventually, my sight became clearer and I could begin to make out the shape standing near the wall. The shadow began to move toward me, and as it did, I noticed that it was more than just a dark outline. It had a face with full features: eyes, ears, nose, mouth, and lips. It had arms, hands, and fingers. It even had legs. But strangely enough, these limbs ran down only as far as the kneecaps and then faded into nothingness. I expected feet to appear as the apparition drew closer, but nothing more materialized.

"And then the horror...:

"As this specter leaned toward the head of my bed, I saw its full face in the pale light reflected through the window.

"It was my own! I felt as if I was looking into a fun-house mirror at some church carnival. The face was mine in content and feature, but the expression was one of sick and sad despair.

"In my terror, I could only look at this creature for a few seconds. I covered my eyes and turned my head away toward the wall, hoping and wishing that I'd wake from this wicked nightmare. I eventually got the courage to turn back again, peeking carefully below the crook of my elbow. I held my breath and opened my eyes once more—it was gone."

"The next thing I remember was the early morning sun filtering through the window. I found myself still in bed, clutching the corners of my pillow like the handrail of a roller coaster."

Pap shuddered a little, as if he was trying to shake the dream from last night out of his head. He seemed agitated that he had allowed himself to remember so much of his vision in such great detail.

Wendy broke the spell that Pap's story had cast. "Good thing it was only a dream," she said reassuringly.

"Yes, good thing," Pap responded with much less confidence.

"What do you think it meant?" Jake wondered.

"Well, some people believe that when you see an image of yourself, it means you're going to die. Maybe that's what I saw last night."

Aaron stepped forward, quite agitated. "Pap—the Fetch! There's no way you saw it last night—no way!"

Aaron's grandfather's eyes got big. A chill went through Wendy and Jake, even though they had no idea what Aaron was talking about.

"How do you know about the Fetch?" Pap was very firm and direct in his questioning.

Aaron answered very matter-of-factly, "It's in the book. I read about it in the guidebook."

"You seem to remember much—much more than I ever thought a boy your age would be able to retain from the book."

"Well, I've got a great teacher," Aaron replied cheerfully.

"Don't get cute with me," Pap warned with a tone that was both impressed with and suspicious of Aaron's knowledge; "It's very unlikely that you'd be able to absorb the subtleties of Folkteller art so quickly, even if you'd read the book a hundred times."

"Pap"—Aaron smiled oddly—"you worry too much."

"Do I?" Pap answered as he tried to look deep into Aaron's eyes. But the teen turned away, as if he was shielding himself from his grandfather's gaze.

Just then, Aaron, Jake, Wendy, and Pap heard the front door creak open. They all wondered who had just entered the unlocked door. Everyone froze for a minute as they listened. They could hear a pair of squeaky tennis shoes rub against the hardwood floors like the rough palm of a circus clown against a twisted animal balloon. They could feel the footsteps echo through the hallway, beating like a telltale heart.

"P-Pap," Wendy stuttered, "you're not expecting anyone, are you?"

"No, I'm not," Pap replied in a hushed tone as he listened more intently.

All eyes were fixed upon the library doorway. The footsteps grew louder and louder until a strange shadow crossed the threshold of the library, announcing the arrival of the mysterious visitor.

"Hey, everybody, sorry I'm late," said a familiar voice.

"Aaron...," Pap rasped in disbelief.

Wendy and Jake were stunned. They couldn't utter a word and just stood there, staring at the person in the doorway and then back at his unbelievable twin, already in the room.

Aaron's grandfather instinctively ran to his desk and fumbled to open the drawer. But before he could get his key into the ancient keyhole, a strange and horrible thing happened.

The creature that everyone thought was the real Aaron spun around on the tapestry carpet. It grinned like a snake that had just swallowed a squealing mouse whole. And then it looked up directly at the ceiling. It opened its mouth wider than humanly possible. Two sets of black, spindly fingers emitted out of the hole in Aaron's face and pushed down upon the sides of his cheeks. The hands continued to push down and wriggle out of the boy's skin, like a child would shed his damp snow pants after hours out in the cold. Within moments, the creature was fully exposed in all of its shadowy, distorted blackness, as its imposturous skin lay in folds upon the floor.

Aaron's grandfather had managed to get the key into the lock and retrieve the book. But before he could do anything else, the wraith shot up toward the ceiling, circled the room three times, and disappeared into the west wall. It was gone.

"Holy mackerel!" was the only thing Jake could utter.

"What the heck just happened?!" Aaron wondered as he still stood in the doorway.

Wendy didn't say a word. She ran over to Aaron and began tugging on his face.

"Ow! Cut that out! What's with you?!" Aaron tried to shoo Wendy away with a wave of his hand as he ducked her advances.

"I need to be sure it's you!" Wendy screamed.

"It's me! It's me! I promise!" Aaron tried to reassure her.

Aaron's grandfather walked over to the leather sofa and plopped down, exhausted. "Children, it appears that the Shadow People have upped their game. Their pursuit of the book is relentless."

"You think?" Jake said sarcastically.

"I've seen their tricks before, but never anything like this," Pap continued with a concerned look on his face.

"We only have an hour before the Transit opens up again. And I'm sure that they're not done with us yet."

"What can we do until then?" Wendy asked with even greater concern.

"We watch and wait," Pap replied, "and above all else, keep the book handy…"

24
Boomerang

The next hour took forever. Pap and Aaron spent the time leafing through the guidebook and talking quietly together.

"How will I ever learn all of this, Pap?" Aaron sighed.

"All in good time, my boy, all in good time," Pap reassured him. "It's taken me this long to learn everything that I know, and it never stops. Everything is an opportunity to learn, and everyone is a teacher, if you let them into your life. The trick is to listen when it's time to listen, speak when you need to speak, and act when the moment arises—that's how you will learn."

Aaron didn't say anything. He just nodded and decided to listen for now.

Every once in a while, Pap and Aaron looked up to find Jake and Wendy engaged in a very different conversation.

"At least it won't be a long trip back," Jake gulped, trying to avoid the obvious.

"Yeah, we got here pretty quickly, so the journey back shouldn't take much longer, I hope," Wendy replied softly.

"I—I just want you to know…" Jake stumbled over his words.

"Yes?" Wendy's head lifted until her eyes met his.

Jake fumbled for the right words, "Um, well, it's just going to be d-different—different when you're gone—that's all."

"I know, Jake. I know what you mean." Wendy held Jake's hand and squeezed it a little.

Tension filled the room as everyone's thoughts and emotions swirled around for different reasons. But no one lost sight of their real focus—to get Wendy home safely. And no one was more focused than Johann Anderson. He knew what was at stake, and he knew the danger involved.

In their quiet discussion, Pap was instructing Aaron how to hold off the Shadow People. He knew that to get Wendy into the Transit safely, they'd have to ward off the dark entities long enough for her to make an escape.

The minute hand on the grandfather clock was almost covering the number 11, while the hour hand closed in on the number 4. The time was drawing near. Aaron's grandfather called Jake and Wendy over to meet with Aaron and himself. As the group huddled together, you could hear muffled whispers and chatter accompanied with subtle hand gestures and finger-pointing in various directions. The house was eerily quiet. It was as if the ticking of the clock had become the heartbeat of the entire structure. Its rhythmic ticking seemed to stress that something was about to happen.

Then it did.

As Pap and the teenagers stood huddled together by the leather sofa, the room suddenly grew very dark. The light from the outside window hadn't changed at all, but inside, everyone watched as thin, veiled shadows began to slither up the walls.

"Now!" Pap yelled.

On Johann Anderson's cue, Jake, Wendy, and Aaron all took their places, forming a semicircle around Pap and the book. They were bound and determined to protect the book and get Wendy home safely.

But then something unexpected happened. They had expected the Shadow People to attack like they had before. They had braced themselves for a direct attack, either on their bodies or even by possession. But that didn't happen.

Instead, the shadows continued to climb up the walls until they had blanketed the room in complete darkness, snuffing out the afternoon sun. Jake ran over to the wall switch to turn on the lights. The lights flickered, dimmed for a minute, and then went out completely.

"Rats!" Jake shouted in frustration as he ran back over to the group.

"What happening?" Wendy asked out loud in fear and confusion.

"I don't know," Pap replied ominously, "but we have to stay close together."

The room continued to get darker, if that was even possible. Pretty soon, it was pitch-black in the library. Jake couldn't see Aaron, even though he was only a few feet away. Wendy couldn't see Pap, even though he was standing right next to her by the sofa. No one could see a thing.

But they could hear things. What they heard weren't sounds of comfort and warmth. No, these sounds were more of the grave. They included the cold flow of damp, swampy air, complete with the aroma of mold and mildew and the faint stench of something dead. The foul wind swept around each of them, brushing up against their bodies as if it was taunting them to do something.

Jake began to swing wildly at the air, trying in vain to punch one of the creatures in its nonexistent face.

"Jake, stand still!" Pap ordered. Even though he couldn't see the boy, he could tell by his sound and motion exactly what he was doing.

Pap ordered everyone to huddle close together, as he clutched the guidebook tightly in his hands. He knew that was what the Shadow People had come for. What he couldn't understand was why they just didn't attack him directly. At this point, it didn't matter. Johann Anderson knew that he had to do something. So, in the deep blackness of the cold room, Pap slowly opened the book. No one saw him do it, but he did.

Jake, Wendy, and Aaron were standing right next to Pap, but they had no idea that he was leafing through the Folkteller Guidebook right in front of their eyes. It seemed preposterous to try and read from the pages while immersed in utter darkness, but Pap did. He did because he knew something about the book that no one else knew.

Some of the pages had been written in braille. For those of you who don't know, braille is a system of writing used by people who can't see. There have been a few Folktellers over the course of time who were blind. All of their entries were written in braille.

Lucis Islip was one of these authors. Strangely enough, Lucis was also the Folkteller who had enabled the illumination of each page of the book by simply reciting his braille entry from the guidebook:

Out of darkness, into light
Bring these words into my sight.
Of stories new and stories old
Those unread must yet be told.

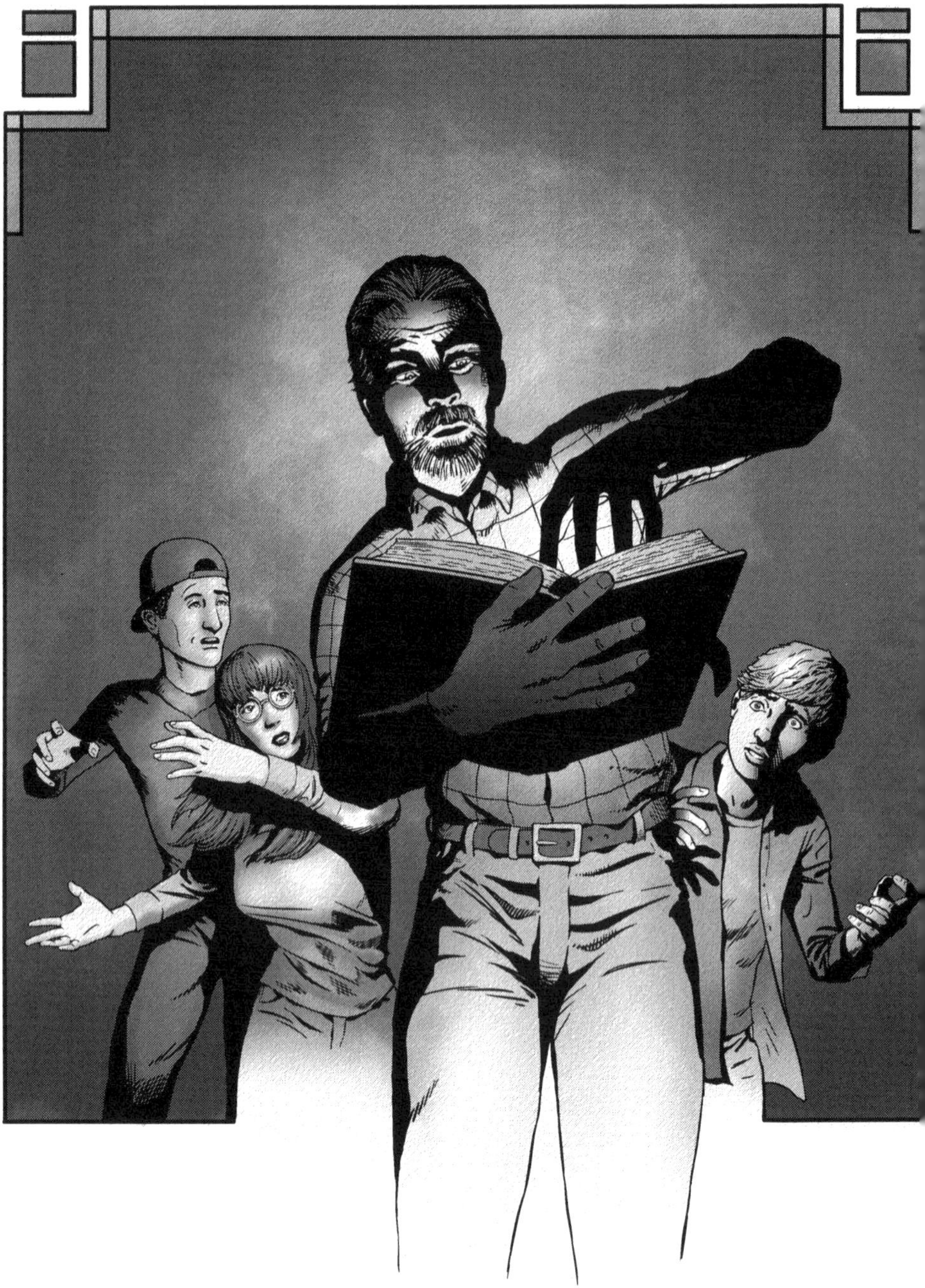

Aaron's grandfather ran his index finger along the raised bumps on the page and recited the words. As the words came out of his mouth, the pages from the book began to burst forth with light, the sudden brightness of which burned their eyes.

Jake, Wendy, and Aaron covered their faces and screamed. They didn't know if this powerful light was the work of the Shadow People or something else.

"It's okay," Pap reassured them as he held the book up over his head. "I just used an illumination poem to brighten things up a bit."

As Pap pivoted the book around the room, he was able to throw light in every corner of the library. The Shadow People stopped their circling and swirling and slipped back between the dark cracks in the bookshelves and floorboards.

"How did you do that?" Aaron wondered as his eyes adjusted to new light in the room.

"Remind me that we need to start you on braille lessons once we're done here today," Pap answered with a sly grin on his face.

With that, Johann Anderson placed the illumined book on a side table so that the entire room was bathed in an even light.

"Look!" Wendy shouted as she pointed to the grandfather clock. "It's open!"

Wendy was right. In the darkness, the glass case of the clock magically swung open, and the familiar whooshing sound from the Transit could be heard within the dark, wooden case.

The full moon had come, and the door back to Wendy's world was open.

"Wendy, you need to go—now!" Johann Anderson's voice was strong and adamant. "There's no time; they'll be coming back at any minute."

Wendy didn't move. She just stood there, not knowing what to do next. Going home had been on her mind ever since she landed in Pap's library. But now, with the moment at hand, she couldn't bring herself to leave.

"Wendy," came a gentle voice from over her shoulder, "you really need to go, right now. I'll miss you, but I'd rather have you safe at home than battling Shadow People here. We'll be fine, I promise."

"Oh, Jake!" Wendy began to sob and buried her face between his chest and shoulder.

"C'mon, Wendy, we promised we wouldn't do this," Jake was trying to stay calm and cool, but he could feel his cheeks burning red as the tears welled up in the corners of his eyes.

"Jake's right, Wendy—you gotta go!" Aaron tried to pry Wendy and Jake apart as gently as possible.

It was right then that the light in the room began to flicker. The Shadow People were nowhere to be seen, until Aaron looked over at the side table, where the guidebook lay wide open—unprotected.

"Pap!" Aaron yelled, but it was too late.

Two sets of spidery fingers had pushed through the top of the table from underneath. It looked like the ink-black tentacles of an octopus breaking the surface of a deep, dark ocean. The slimy digits wrapped slowly around the book and constricted it shut—snuffing out most of the light from the entire room.

Jake instinctively pushed Wendy away, turned her around, and guided her rather roughly toward the open clock cabinet. "Sorry, Wendy, but it's time!" Jake exhaled as he inched her along the carpet.

Once Pap saw the shadowy hands grab hold of the book, he leaped for the table. No one had ever seen him move like that before, including himself. His arms, torso, and legs stretched in a full, strained extension, but it was no use. He grunted with a painful, primal yawp as his twisted body missed its target and fell with a heavy whump onto the floor.

Johann Anderson lay there, like a well-dressed sack of Idaho potatoes, completely unconscious.

There was only a tiny light left in the room, emitting from the edges of the closed guidebook, wrapped in the shadowy clutches of one of the creatures.

It was Aaron's turn to leap for the book. He couldn't think of anything else to do in that moment. Pap was down, Jake was too far away, and Wendy was about to enter the Transit.

Without another thought, Aaron took one step over his grandfather and flew into the air. Time seemed to slow down as Aaron launched himself toward the floating book that had already started to move away from the side table. As if by instinct, Aaron's outstretched hands aimed for the sliver of light between the pages of the Folkteller's Guidebook.

With as much force as possible, Aaron grabbed the leather binding with both hands and pulled it toward his chest. The shadow's grip never loosened. Worse than that, once the teen touched the book, it was like a million needles penetrated his skin. His hands burned like the fire of a thousand flames, yet he never let go.

Time seemed to speed up to normal again. Aaron did a shoulder roll onto the hardwood floor and flipped back up to his feet. The inertia of this maneuver flung the shadow beast against the far wall of the library, where it briefly oozed back into a shelf of books.

Johann Anderson's grandson stood up straight and tall. There was a hissing that emanated from all four walls, as if the books were rasping a tortured message. They all heard it, except Pap, who remained motionless on the floor.

"Get the Fleshhhhhh..." was the horrible hiss that sickened the very air in the room.

Before anyone had the chance to respond or answer, the darkness returned in full force. The walls closed in and surrounded everyone in the room. Jake, Wendy, and Aaron felt like they were slowly being swallowed by an invisible, foul-smelling beast.

Wendy cried out in the clos- ing darkness, "Aaron, over here! Throw it over here!"

Aaron did not hesitate. He felt compelled to throw the Folkteller's Guidebook atced in a beam of traveling light as it trailed through the air. The darkness seemed to be quite aware that the book had left Aaron's hands. The shadows closed in even faster, as if they were trying to gulp down the room whole.

The guidebook was headed straight toward the grandfather clock. Wendy knew it, as she was standing right there. The book landed squarely in her waiting hands. Once it was secure against her body, Wendy ducked into the open clock cabinet.

Suddenly a beam of moonlight pierced the darkness, burning directly into the cabinet. The door slammed shut, the brief shaft of light was consumed by the thick blackness, and Wendy vanished.

There was a brief whooshing, sucking sound like a vacuum hose that had just unclogged itself of a brief obstruction.

Wendy was gone, along with the precious guidebook.

But the Shadow People hadn't left. On the contrary, once they realized that the book had gone through the Transit, their behavior became much more violent. Like an evil cyclone, all of the darkness in the room swarmed around itself, forming a narrow vortex of blackness. This terrifying tornado shot into the clock cabinet in rapid pursuit of Wendy and the Folkteller's Guidebook.

This fact became even clearer as the spinning shadows slammed into the back of the grandfather clock. The Transit was closed to them, which sent dark spirits flying backward in all directions. It looked as if a giant truck tire had sped through a deep, thick mud puddle. Shadow People were flung about the room like muck splattered on a pale, white wall.

As the light was slowly seeping back into the room, Jake and Aaron looked at each other in delayed shock.

Wendy was gone.

Pap was unconscious.

There was no longer any book to protect them. Worst of all, though the Shadow People were stunned, they were still very angry and not going away.

The teens slid closer to each other.

"Wh-what happens next?" Jake stuttered.

"I don't know," Aaron answered as his head swiveled around the room, looking for the first dark wraith to return. "But whatever happens, we're not going down without a fight."

25
The Seer

As predicted, the timeless specters had not disappeared for good. They began to shoot out of the walls and floor with even greater speed and determination.

Without warning, they circled both Jake and Aaron in a blurry black mass of foul wind and shadow.

"The air!" Jake yelled above the whooshing wind that enveloped him. "Can't breathe!"

Aaron was having the same reaction to the spinning shadows. The vortex that they created around the teenagers was spinning so fast that it was sucking all of the oxygen out of the air. Jake and Aaron were suffocating.

The teens were locked in place, unable to move within the eye of this horrible hurricane. Jake dropped to his knees as the lack of oxygen made him weak and wobbly.

Aaron watched his friend fall down to the floor. He knew that in a few minutes he'd pass out from asphyxiation. His mind was spinning just as fast as the vortex around him.

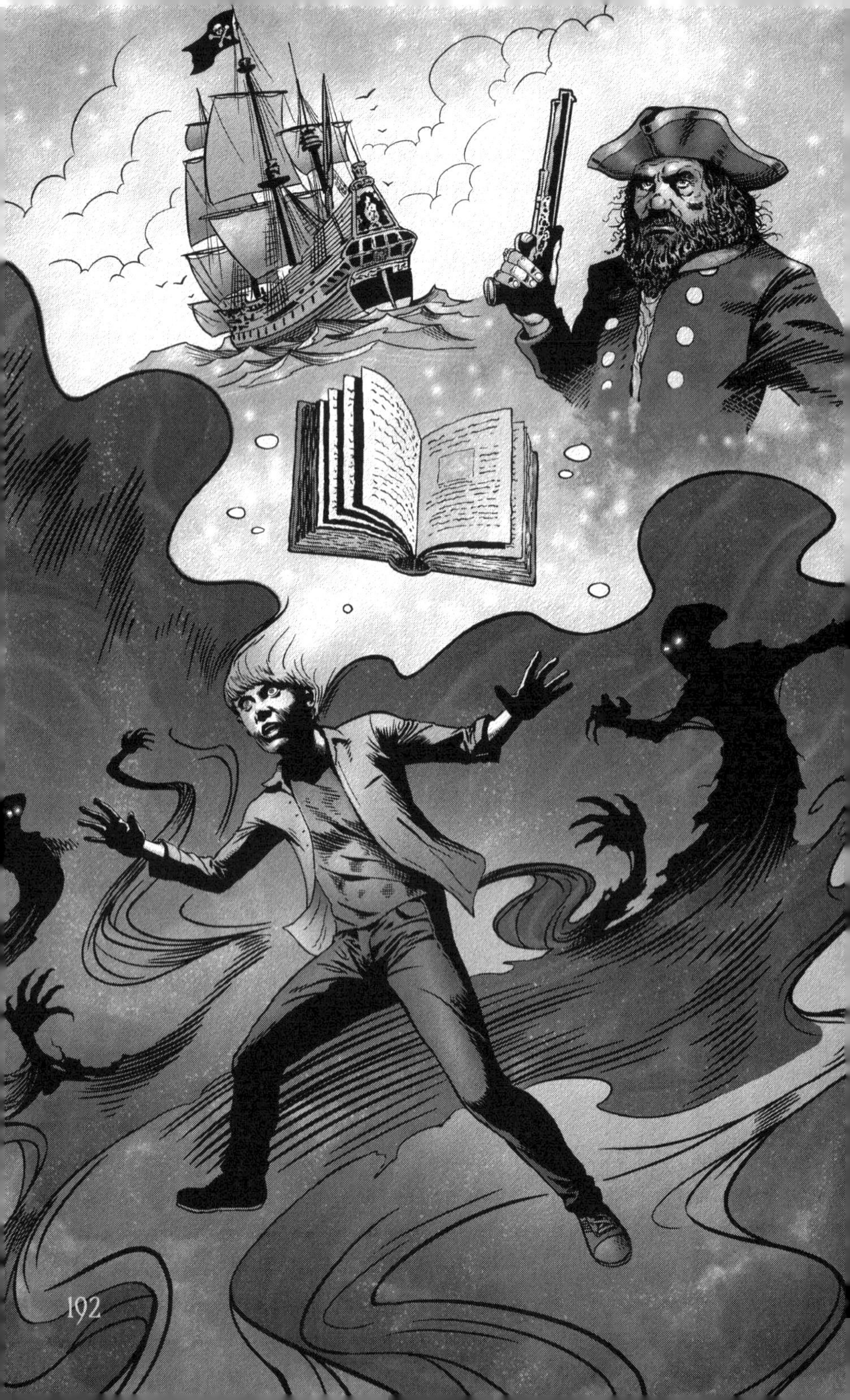

Then something peculiar happened. It was right at that moment, just before he was going to fall for the last time, that something strange and wonderful occurred.

As his eyes closed, Aaron's mind began to clear. The spinning stopped, and in his mind's eye he could see the book. The Folkteller's Guidebook—it was right in front of his face!

Somehow—he had no idea how he was doing it—Aaron opened the book with his mind. He could see all the pages as clearly as if he was holding the real book right in his hands. Instinctively, the book flipped to the section of never-ending stories. Aaron found the page he wanted and began speaking out loud with the last breath in his body:

Captain Jack sat around the campfire with his fellow pirates...

The words came out dry and raspy at first. The more Aaron spoke, the weaker the wind became.

He looked to his first mate and commanded him to tell them all a wondrous story of pirate adventures...

It was working. The vortex was slowing down.

The first mate obliged. He stood before his captain, his mates, and the roaring fire and began his story...

As the force of the Shadow People diminished, Jake and Aaron could breathe better. Jake looked over at Aaron with a confused look. "What's going on? How are you doing that?"

Aaron didn't respond; he just kept on with his recitation. And the more Aaron spoke, the fewer Shadow People there were. They were retreating back into their timeless darkness. But they weren't going away quietly.

As the black specters spun out of the vortex and back into the walls, they seemed to hiss something. With terrible anger, fear, and frustration, they wheezed out a single, panicked word from their unseen throats. Over and over again they rasped:

"Seer…Seer…Seer…!"

After a few minutes, it was over. The Shadow People were gone. Everything was quiet, and Aaron and Jake were the only ones left in the room. Or so they thought. In all of the commotion, they had completely forgotten about Pap.

They heard moaning in the corner of the room.

"Pap!" Aaron yelled as he stumbled over to his grandfather. Johann Anderson's grandson was still a little light-headed and jelly-legged from his battle with the Shadow People, but he was more concerned for his grandfather. Both teens found their way to where Pap was lying. He was stirring in a hazy stupor as he tried to sit up.

"Pap, don't." Jake slid his body behind Aaron's grandfather, in an effort to hold the old man in a more stable sitting position.

"Wh-what happened? Where am I?" Pap stuttered. "A-and where's, where's the book?" He tried in vain to get up on his feet. With arms flopping weakly and legs refusing to respond to his mental commands, Johann Anderson looked like a newborn foal. His wonky, wobbly knees almost knocked together as he struggled to gain his footing. But it was no use; he was completely helpless as he fell back into Jake's waiting arms.

"Pap, take it easy," Aaron said calmly. "The book is gone. I threw it to Wendy just before she disappeared into the Transit."

Pap thought for a minute and then asked quietly, "So Wendy has the book?"

"Yes, Pap, Wendy has the book," Jake replied.

"That's good... It's good that she has it... Very good..." Pap seemed to be consoling himself as his senses returned. He was just beginning to process all that had happened while he was knocked out.

"Something else happened, Pap. Something weird," Aaron began. "The Shadow People came after us after Wendy disappeared. Just before they sucked the life out of us, I started seeing things. I could see the Folkteller's Guidebook in my head."

"Really, my boy?" Johann Anderson looked intrigued

as he pushed off of Jake, trying to straighten up. "What did you see exactly?"

"I saw everything," Aaron answered plainly. "It was like the guidebook had been imprinted in my brain. I could turn each page with my mind. I could even go to any section I wanted with just a flick of my thoughts."

Jake broke into the conversation. "The Shadow People freaked out once Aaron started reciting a never-ending story. But the weirdest thing was what they were saying as they flew away. They kept repeating—Seer, Seer, Seer."

"They said that? Are you sure?" Pap wondered.

"They did..." Jake's eyes were as wide as the moon. Johann Anderson swiveled his head back toward his grandson. "Is this true, Aaron? Is that what they were saying?"

"I think so. At least that's what it sounded like. What does that mean?"

Pap got up slowly, leaning on Jake for support until he was standing completely upright. With one hand firmly on the edge of his desk he regained his composure.

"Aaron, the Shadow People are liars. They use their lies and deceptions to foster their evil plans; it's a part of their nature. But the one thing they can't lie about is the light of truth. When they see it, they fear it and must call it by name."

"What are you saying, Pap? Are you all right?"

"If they called you a Seer, then you must be one." Pap's tone was serious.

"What the heck is a Seer anyway?" Jake asked.

Johann Anderson looked at Jake and then back at Aaron, addressing them both at the same time. "Throughout time, there have only been a handful of Seers. They retain all of our Folkteller knowledge within their hearts and minds…

"Seers *are* the guidebook."

26
Home Again

Wendy tumbled out of the broom closet into the first-floor hallway. The moonlight that flooded the Transit disappeared as the portal closed in upon itself.

She was dizzy and disoriented from her spinning journey through the Transit, but she was still in one piece. As she picked herself up off the floor, she felt heavy, like a piece of steel held down by a magnet. Wendy realized that she was still clinging that tightly to the Folkteller's Guidebook.

She looked up at the side-mounted clock above the hallway. It read 2:40 p.m. That was pretty close to the time that Wendy, Pap, Aaron, and Jake had escaped into the closet almost a month ago.

Wendy continued to get her bearings, wondering if any time had really passed. Had she arrived right back at the moment she left? Pap had said that would happen, but maybe it was all a dream? Okay, but how could it be a dream—she had the guidebook right in her hands! Thoughts like these kept swirling around Wendy's head as more came flooding in.

It was right then that she felt a gentle but firm hand grasp her shoulder. "I'm glad to see you made it back…and with the book too."

Wendy froze in her tracks. Her instincts made her want to whip around to see who it was or just run in the other direction. She didn't do either. Instead, she clutched the book closely and asked quietly, "What do you want?"

Thankfully, the next sound she heard was a kind, familiar voice saying, "It's me, honey; everything's okay now."

Wendy turned around slowly. She looked into the warm, friendly face of her guidance counselor, Mrs. Napp. A feeling of relief and overwhelming emotion washed over Wendy and she fell into Mrs. Napp's lap.

"It's fine now, honey...You're safe and you're home." Mrs. Napp held Wendy firmly and shushed her head sweetly. After a while, Wendy calmed down and Mrs. Napp was able to direct her down the hall and into her office.

The guidance counselor sat Wendy down in a guest chair and got her a cold cup of water. Eventually Wendy was able to think more clearly. As the fog lifted and her old world came into better focus, she looked up at Mrs. Napp and asked, "How did you know?"

Mrs. Napp smiled and stated simply, "Who do you think scheduled the assembly?"

"You did," Wendy answered, as if the gears in her head were grinding a little.

"And who opened the emergency door for you when you ran out to help Mr. Anderson and the boys?"

"You did," Wendy answered again. "But why?"

"Because, honey, we need the book here, and you were the one chosen to retrieve it."

Wendy jumped up from her chair. She grabbed the book off the corner of Mrs. Napp's desk and was about to run out the door. After falling for Aaron's doppelganger, she wasn't sure who she could trust anymore.

Mrs. Napp didn't flinch. She didn't even try to stop Wendy from bolting out of her office.

"Dear, it's okay if you want to leave," the counselor said calmly. "But you should know that you can never run away from yourself."

"What the heck is that supposed to mean?" Wendy was angry now. She turned around to face Mrs. Napp. "I'm not running away from anyone or anything. I'm just trying to protect the book!"

"Wendy, there's no need for that. The book is supposed to be here."

"How do you know?" Wendy asked defiantly.

"Well," Mrs. Napp responded with an air of sincere seriousness, "how else are we supposed to begin *your* apprenticeship?"

27
The Lost Girl

Jake felt like he had been turned inside out. Everything had happened so fast: Wendy disappeared with the book, Pap got injured, and now Aaron was some all-seeing freak who had a photographic memory. And then there was Jake: same old, plain old Jake. He felt like he'd lost everything as he stood next to Aaron and Pap in the aftermath of their epic battle.

It was clear that Aaron's grandfather was going to need some medical attention. Though he could sit up okay, Pap couldn't stand up on his feet for long. Something was bruised or broken, and Aaron was soon on the phone with his parents, letting them know that they needed help.

As Jake watched over Pap while Aaron contacted his family, he could feel his emotions creeping back in. There was a sinking, dull thud in the pit of his stomach, an emptiness that drained down from his heart and

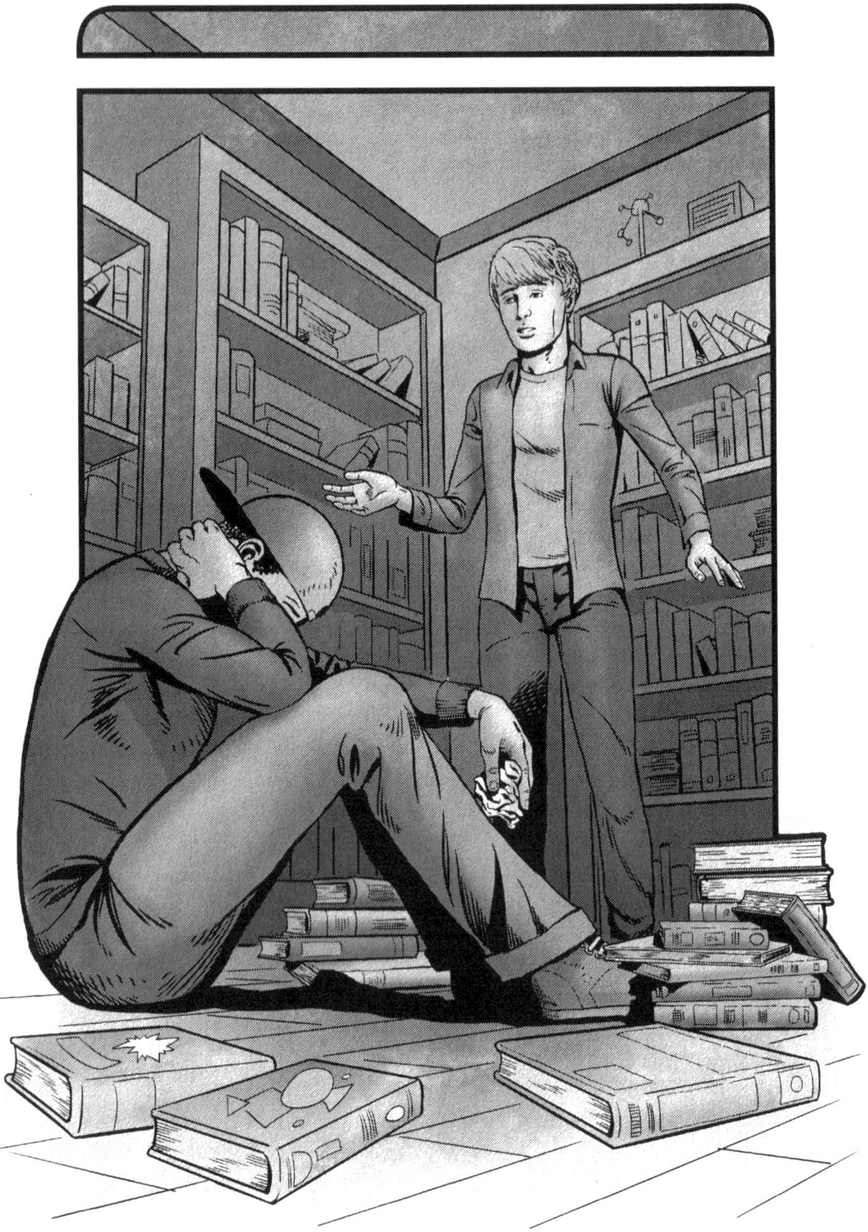

into his gut. As the world settled down around him, he remembered that he had just lost the girl he loved.

Wendy was gone. Gone forever. Jake could feel his throat tighten, and he swallowed hard, as if he was trying to keep all of his emotions down in his gut. But the thoughts and feelings wouldn't relent. They welled up inside of him and flooded his entire body with an uncomfortable heat.

Jake took off his coat in a desperate attempt to relieve himself from the feverish feeling. As he was pulling his arms out from his coat sleeves, he noticed a folded slip of paper crammed into the inside pocket. He finished taking off his coat and set it on the couch, then grabbed the note out of the pocket.

It was a simple sheet of plain white notepaper, folded a few times to make an off-centered square. Jake unfolded the note to reveal Wendy's familiar handwriting. He took a deep breath and read:

Hi Jake, it's ME!

If you're reading this note, I'm probably already gone. We knew this was going to happen and I know we agreed to no long goodbyes.

But I just had to tell you how much I'm going to miss you. You're sweet, funny, and you just make me feel special whenever I'm around you. I'll miss your laughter, your dumb jokes, and the awkward way you hold my hand.

I'll never forget you, no matter what happens. Though we have to live our lives apart, we'll always be together.

This isn't goodbye forever, just goodbye for now. Stay sweet and know that I love you. Keep smiling!

Love, Wendy

"She loves me," Jake whispered. "Wendy said she loves me. Incredible."

Jake could feel the heat leaving his body from the hot tears that rolled down his face. He felt like he was floating through space for what seemed like an eternity. There were no thoughts, just the numb emptiness of what he had lost and the echo of Wendy's words: *This isn't goodbye forever, just goodbye for now...*

Jake swallowed the bitter tears, bad medicine for a broken heart.

"Hey, what's wrong with you?" A familiar voice shattered Jake's thoughts as he hid the damp drops on his cheeks.

"Um—uh, nothing, nothing's wrong, why?" Jake steadied himself.

"Well, because you're wiping your face with a crumpled note in your hand," Aaron answered, trying to break the tension.

"It's nothing…Just a note Wendy left me."

"Oh." Aaron's voice was much softer now. "Sorry, man, I didn't know…"

"No worries." Jake did his best to fake his feelings. He didn't want Aaron to know how much that note meant to him. But Aaron was Jake's best friend—he already knew and was willing to just leave it at that. There were no more questions.

Right then, they heard the creaky front door open.

"Aaron, where are you?!"

"Mom, we're in here, in the library!" Aaron yelled back.

Within a few seconds, Ana and Jason Anderson entered the library and went right over to where Pap was sitting. Aaron had told them about the battle with the Shadow People, but without all the details.

"Is everyone okay?" Aaron's dad asked seriously.

"Where's Wendy?" Aaron's mom looked around the room with great concern.

"She went back home," Jake said flatly as he pointed to the grandfather clock.

"Oh," Aaron's mom said sheepishly. "Well, I guess that's a good thing, then…"

With that, Ana and Jason tended to Aaron's grandfather. Pap insisted that he would be fine, but that didn't matter. He was going to be taken to the hospital to be checked out. Aaron's mom and dad had made their decision, and nothing was going to sway them.

Despite Pap's complaining, they helped him gather his things and pulled his coat over his shoulders before they took him out to the car.

Aaron and Jake were relieved. Finally, someone else had arrived to take control of the situation. They were tired, hungry, and emotionally drained.

It was over. It was finally over.

28
A Nail Hole

Pap was going to be fine. But his days of Transit travel were over. The doctors had discovered that outside of his bumps and bruises from the battle, Johann Anderson suffered from a congenital heart defect. It was something that had been there since birth, but it was just discovered when they examined him at the hospital. The stress of folktelling, traveling to other dimensions, and warding off Shadow People had made it worse.

Aaron and his family quietly crossed the threshold into Pap's hospital room. He had been given some medication to help him sleep, and everyone was trying their best not to wake him. It was sad to see Pap lying there so helplessly. But at least he was still with them.

Aaron's mom, dad, and brother Marty each said a few words to Pap and watched him for a while. Eventually everyone was ready to leave.

"Aaron, are you coming? Let's let Pap get some rest," his dad said to him as they were leaving the room.

"Just a minute, Dad," Aaron answered quietly. "I'll just be a minute."

Pap's grandson went back to his bedside and touched his grandfather's head gently. Slowly, Johann Anderson's eyes opened.

"Ahoy, my boy…" Pap's voice trailed out of his mouth with a raspy rattle.

"Pap, it's me," Aaron replied as he smiled down upon his grandfather. "How are you feeling?"

"I've felt better," Pap whispered, "but I'll continue to improve as time goes by."

Aaron smiled again, reassuring the old man that he believed him.

"Aaron"—Pap spoke more clearly this time—"I'm retired. You're in charge now. You must carry on the family trade."

The teen didn't know what to say. He'd thought that this day would come, but not so soon—he wasn't ready to be a full-fledged Folkteller.

"But Pap, I—I'm not ready. Not yet."

Pap smiled weakly and then grabbed Aaron's wrist with a grip that was more powerful than expected. "Your name, Aaron, means 'high mountain'… and so you must begin your climb. Don't worry—I'm not leaving, not just yet. I'll be here to help."

"But I just don't know, Pap. I mean…"

Pap's grip grew firmer, and his eyes widened as they looked directly into Aaron's own eyes. "Boy, your destiny, your dreams, and your ambitions are like a tiny nail hole in a wall that you've never noticed before. It could be right next to you for your whole life and you may never see it. Others will deny that it's even there. They'll tell you're crazy, it's all in your head, there's nothing there. But if you search and strive and seek out that little, tiny hole, you'll find it. And when you find it, that almost invisible speck on the wall will grow."

Pap took a long breath and then continued. "As you draw closer, that pinpoint will become a peephole, where you can see your future far ahead. The more you look, the more you will see, and feel, and experience.

Before long, that hole in the wall will become a window, and then an entryway with a door, that only you can open. And when you finally find that door, you'll be more than ready to walk right on through."

With that, Johann Anderson released his grip on his grandson. He had said what he needed to say.

The rest was up to Aaron.

29
A New Book

Aaron opened the front door and yelled, "Pap, it's me!" From a hidden room inside the old house he heard, "Ahoy, my boy! Come in and see me!"

These words were music to the boy's ears. For a moment, it was as if the whole nightmare had never happened and things were as they once were. As Aaron walked across the familiar floor, he imagined Pap sitting in the library as he had done for so many years, waiting for his young grandson with snacks and stories.

But it was not to be. Aaron turned the corner and found the library empty. His heart sank as he continued down the hall and up the stairs toward Pap's bedroom. He stepped inside and found his favorite grandfather sitting up in bed, looking paler, thinner, and frailer than before.

Aaron took a deep breath and pursed his lips. He was resolved to keep his smile on and his attitude bright. He owed Pap that much, at least.

"Hey, Pap, how are you feeling?" Aaron asked with all of the good cheer he could muster

"If I felt any better, I'd have to be two people," Pap replied with a weak smile.

"Do you mind if I look around in the library for a while?" his grandson asked quietly but with deep respect.

"I wouldn't have it any other way. Now go, and I'll be in after a little while."

With that, Aaron left his grandfather and proceeded back down the stairs, across the hall, and into the library. The whole room seemed different now. It was as if the light and energy of the place had been snuffed out. All that was left was the heavy dust of old books and the faint, lingering peppermint of Pap's hard candy that he always kept in a glass dish on the side table.

Despite the vacant, empty feeling, Aaron was still drawn to the room. He began to scan the shelves and tables for books that he'd never read before. His eyes moved up and down, then back and forth, as he read spine after spine of familiar volumes. It wasn't until his gaze reached the end of the top shelf of books that his eyes stopped.

There was something. It was something he'd never seen before. It looked like an old, weathered, leather-bound book with a big, brass clasp holding it closed. Aaron stepped up on a rolling library ladder that Pap used for the higher shelves. He slid gracefully over to the end of the bookshelf. He climbed up the steps and retrieved the tome from its nestled resting place between Dickens and Twain.

There was no title on the spine, no author either. As the teenager sat on the floor, he clicked the unlocked clasp and opened the creaky cover. Inside he discovered two things: there was a small key attached to the inside cover, and the whole book, hundreds and hundreds of pages, was completely blank.

Aaron thought out loud, "What the heck? Why would Pap keep an old, empty book like this?"

"So you can fill it!" came a weak voice from the doorway.

Aaron spun around to see his grandfather standing on the threshold of the library in his green plaid bathrobe.

"What do you mean, 'fill it'? Fill it with what?" Aaron wondered.

"Now, don't be dim." Pap dismissed Aaron's question. "You know exactly what I'm talking about, boy."

Pap made his way slowly over to his mahogany desk and opened the top drawer. From the drawer, Aaron's grandfather produced a large, old-fashioned ebony box. He handed the box to his grandson, who opened it to reveal a single, magnificent inkwell pen. The pen came complete with a wide assortment of metallic nibs, and three generous bottles of deep indigo ink.

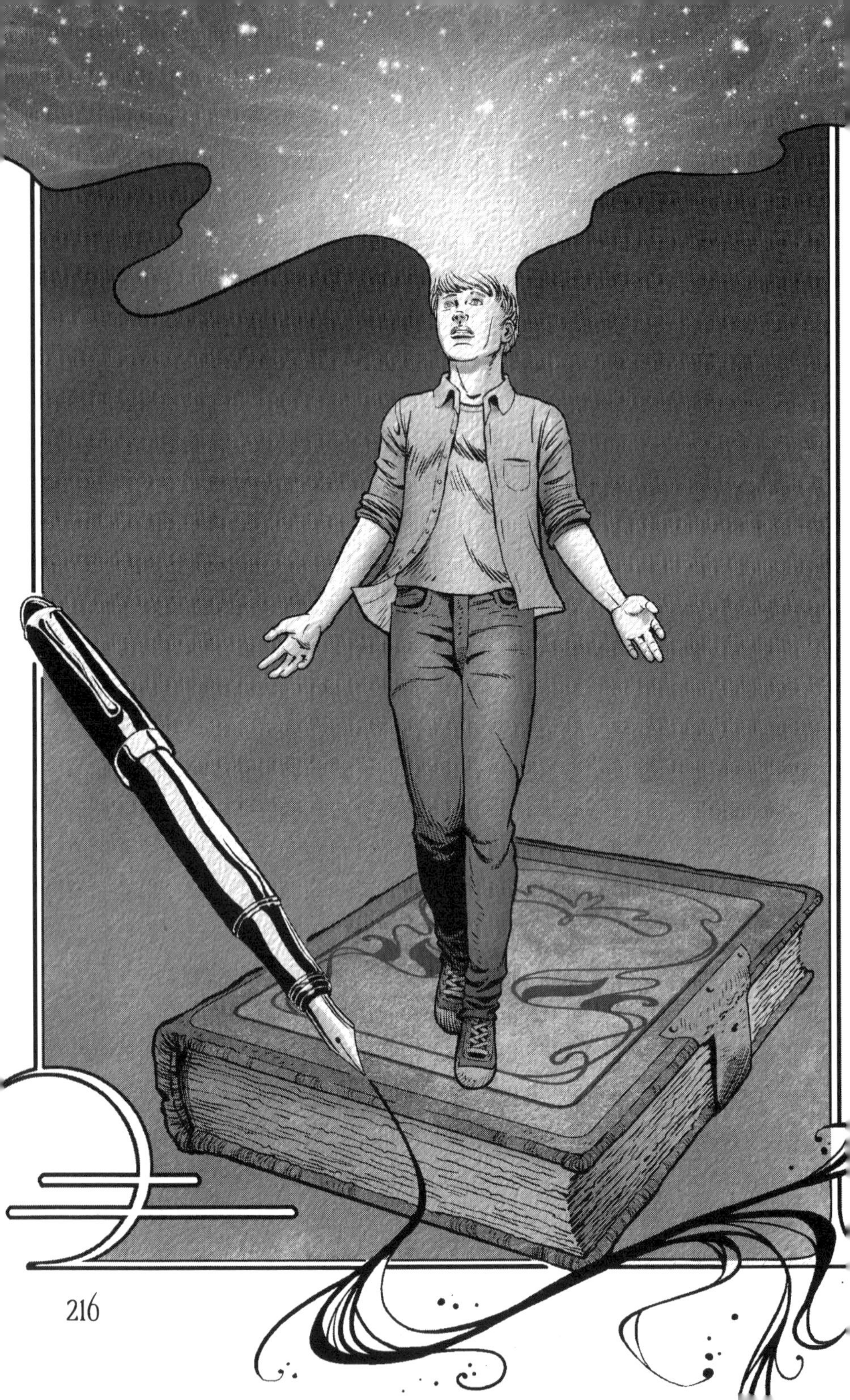

As if by instinct, Aaron slipped one of the fancy nibs into the end of the pen and unscrewed the top of one of the ink bottles. He opened the blank book to the first page and carefully touched the tip of the pen to the upper left-hand corner of the thick paper.

It was right at that moment that something wonderful happened.

As that first, tiny speck of ink bled onto the paper, a strange, electric energy surged through Aaron's entire body. His eyes rolled in the back of his head, and he fell into a strange trance. The boy was unaware that he was sitting on the floor of his grandfather's library anymore. Instead, he was hovering in an empty, white space where there was no sound or sight to be seen. There was only white light and blank space that filtered through his outstretched fingers.

As he floated there in the nothingness, a thought came into his head. It was more than a thought, actually; it was a story. It was a story he remembered reading in the Folkteller's Guidebook. As the story flowed through his brain, Aaron's right arm reached out with his forefinger extended, as if he was pointing at something in the distance. Blindly and blissfully, Aaron's finger began writing in the air with invisible ink on a white light canvas that wasn't really there. His arm went up and down with broad, swooping strokes, like a great conductor leading his magnificent orchestra through the crescendos and valleys of a Rossini symphony.

Then, slowly and calmly, the sensation began to fade. Aaron saw his surroundings fill up with color, shapes, and form again. Soon he realized that he hadn't ever moved at all. He was still sitting on the floor of his grandfather's library with the old book lying flat in his lap. There was only one difference.

The pages weren't blank anymore.

"What just happened?" Aaron's words slowly tumbled out of his mouth in puzzled confusion. "Did I do this?"

"Yes, you did," Johann Anderson said with a knowing smile.

"B-but how?" Aaron stumbled over his words again.

"It's simple, my boy. You are a Seer. And now you're able to document what you see."

"Pap, please tell me what's happening to me." Johann could hear the slight fear and anxiety in Aaron's voice.

Aaron's grandfather walked slowly over to the teen and put his hand on Aaron's shoulder. "Not to worry, Aaron. All is as it should be. What you've just experienced, what has just happened to you, is perfectly normal—for a Seer. You've just been through your first *summoning*."

Aaron furrowed his brow and looked up at his grandfather. "Pap, you know that I've no idea what you're talking about."

"I know, boy," Pap said reassuringly. "Let me explain. Once a Guidebook is lost, stolen, or disappears for any reason, an odd chain of events may occur. Sometimes, the book is lost only temporarily. When that happens, nothing out of the ordinary takes place, and the book is eventually found. But when a Guidebook is truly gone, that's when things get interesting. A lost Guidebook triggers a *summoning* by a chosen Seer. Someone like you, a Seer, begins to have visions and out-of-body experiences. During these sessions, the stories that have been lost are summoned back by the Seer and recorded in a newly written Folkteller's Guidebook."

"Wait a minute." Aaron stopped his grandfather. "You mean to tell me that I'm rewriting the Folkteller's Guidebook?"

"Oh, you're doing much more than that," Pap continued. "You're actually building upon the stories that we've held for centuries. You're adding new notes, thoughts, and ideas to what has already existed. You are creating as you remember. That is what a *summoning* is truly all about."

Aaron was frustrated and angry that he was just learning about this now. "Jeez Pap, maybe tomorrow you'll tell me I can fly or see through walls or something!"

"Don't mock the gifts you've been given, boy. It's ungrateful and dangerous. Summoning is serious business. You'd be well-advised to channel your thoughts properly, and focus on the task as it comes."

"Or what?" Aaron snapped back in unusual fashion. "I didn't ask for any of this. It all just showed up and I got dumped on."

"Very true, my boy, very true," Johan Anderson agreed with his troubled grandson. "I felt the same way when I found out I was a Folkteller. I was just about your age when it happened. Fortunately, my father was one too, so it wasn't as much of a surprise for me. Still, there was a big part of me that resented the fact that this would be my lot in life. I felt like I wasn't even given a choice, and that my life had been planned out for me."

"But you went ahead with it anyway, right?" Aaron questioned.

"I did, yes. At first I told myself I would give it a shot, try out this folktelling thing for a while. My father told me all along it was my choice, so I felt like I had an out if I needed it. I went along with the whole thing for a few months. I even went on a few folktelling journeys with my father."

"So, what made you decide to commit for real?" Aaron asked.

Pap chuckled a little under his breath as he remembered the moment from such a long time ago. "It all became real to me when I was reading a book of famous quotes one day. I came across a section on greatness. For some reason, I was drawn to the simple words of William Shakespeare and Winston Churchill.

Shakespeare told me, 'Be not afraid of greatness: some are born great, some achieve greatness, and others have greatness thrust upon them.' And Churchill added, 'The price of greatness is responsibility.'"

Pap took a deep breath as his beaten, bruised, and tired body reacted to his heightened state. "I don't know what it was about those words, but they rang in my head immediately after that. In fact, they've been echoing around my skull ever since. I never thought I was great, but the powers I had were. So, I knew I had only three choices: one, do nothing with them and move on with my life; two, use my powers for my own selfish interests and exploits, or three, do something good with the gifts I've been given."

Pap sat back on the couch in exhaustion. With a tired yet satisfied smile on his face, he looked down at his favorite grandson and simply said, "I opted for number three."

30
Words Remembered

Johann Anderson's grandson sat silently on the floor for a very long time. He thought about how much his life had changed. No longer was he the happy-go-lucky boy whose life was built on the consistent and commonplace. Gone were the days of root beer, snacks, and stories after school. His past had been demolished by the events of the past few weeks, and he could never get back to that place of innocence and comfort.

Aaron thought of his future prospects. It seemed to him that if he pursued his path of destiny, his rightful place as a Folkteller, then struggle and hardship would be his lot in life. He would be living in a world where the future could never be known. Fear, danger, and even death would be lurking right around the corner. At fourteen years old, that seemed like a really crappy life.

After what seemed like an eternity, just sitting and pondering his existence, the light bulb went on in Aaron's head. He opened his mouth and spoke the words he'd seen but had never spoken before:

"Pap, your heart knows in silence the secrets of the days and the nights. But your ears thirst for the sound of your heart's knowledge…"

The elder Anderson pricked up his ears, astonished at the words he was hearing. "What is this you say, boy?"

"I think I've got it, Pap; I think I do!" Aaron continued excitedly. "Last month, Mom and I were going through my baby book, the one you gave me when I was born. There was a passage you wrote on the inside cover:

"'Your heart knows in silence the secrets of the days and the nights. But your ears thirst for the sound of your heart's knowledge.'

"I never knew what that meant before. But now I know. All along, for all those years, you've been folktelling to me! Your stories, your adventures, and all of the books you've given me—it was all to prepare me for this moment, right?"

Aaron's grandfather didn't answer audibly, but his head nodded slightly, and the expression on his face told his grandson that he was on the right track.

"You were preparing me for this decision, weren't you?" Aaron said with greater clarity.

Pap remained quiet, but still seemed to be communicating to his grandson through facial expressions and slight twitches of his hands.

"It was the stories. It was the stories that revealed what's always been inside of me." Aaron kept talking as if he'd opened a giant trunk of treasures that needed to be emptied. "But you couldn't come right out and tell me, right? Of course you couldn't! I wouldn't have understood at all. I probably would have thought you were off your rocker—nuts!"

Aaron's grandfather gave a wizened smile to his grandson and finally broke his silence. "Such a clever boy. Yes, all of it's true. I have been grooming you for years. Now you're of the age where all that can be revealed is revealed. But in the end you still have to make your own choices. The final decision of what you will do with the rest of your life is solely up to you."

With that, the young man got up from the floor and gave his grandfather a heartfelt and grateful hug. Not another word was spoken. Aaron gathered his things, including his new, incomplete Folkteller's Guidebook, and made his way out of the library toward the front door. As he grabbed the brass doorknob of the giant wooden door, he could hear Pap slowly shuffle into the hallway.

Aaron turned to face his grandfather and heard the faint rasp of Pap's voice say, "Be careful with that book. Now you know the power it possesses. And now you know those who wish to possess it as well."

Aaron nodded and waved his hand back to his grandfather. He then patted the cover of the leather-bound book, acknowledging that he would heed his grandfather's warning.

The young man stepped off of his grandfather's front porch and into the middle of a cloudless day. There was a strange feeling that overcame Aaron. It was as if he had stepped out onto an artist's canvas, where the background and the scenery had been painted already. But in the scene there weren't any people or animals or anything that would illustrate action.

There was only him. And with each movement, each step, each swing of his arm as he walked down the street, the world around him became animated and full of life.

31
Same Difference

The alarm clock rang, a cold steel hammer on his eardrums. Jake rolled over like oatmeal into a lumpy gray morning. On the other side of town, Aaron was going through the same motions, fumbling around in the pre-dawn darkness trying to silence the horrible alarm bells of a school day morning.

After their weekday rituals of showers, cereal, and loading their backpacks, Jake and Aaron met up at their usual street-corner spot.

"Mornin'," Jake mumbled as if still half asleep.

"Hey," Aaron replied as they both turned slowly and made their way on the ordinary path that led them toward school.

It seemed that there wasn't much to say because there was everything to say. How do you begin a conversation when the life that you once knew was completely gone? Here were Jake and Aaron. They'd been friends since middle school, and they'd been walking to school almost as long. Their neighborhood hadn't changed. The houses they passed five days a week all looked as they always did. The streets they walked down were just as narrow and tree-lined as they'd always been. On the outside, everything around them was exactly the same as it had been a few weeks ago. Yet somehow, everything inside of them was different. Life is funny like that: our experiences change us. For good or bad, whatever we go through has a way of twisting and reshaping our hearts, heads, and souls.

All of that weaving and turning seemed to have knotted both boys' tongues. It took almost all of Aaron's energy to break this spell of silence: "Hey, man, I know things seem really weird right now."

"Ya think?" Jake acknowledged with just a hint of sarcasm.

"C'mon, you know what I mean." Aaron elbowed his old friend.

"No, I don't. What do you mean?"

"Jake, you know what I'm talking about. Everything that's happened over the past month!"

"Dude, you're looney. I have no clue what you're talking about," Jake insisted.

Aaron stopped and looked at Jake in earnest. "Are you serious?"

Jake tried to hold back the grin that was spreading across his face.

"No, I'm just bustin' your chops a little." He shoved Aaron back playfully. "What are you gonna do now, use your Folkteller powers on me?"

"Yeah, I'll read you to death," Aaron shot back, smiling.

"Well, that would be a *storied* ending for us all, wouldn't it?"

"Oh, shut up!" Aaron yelled without a hint of seriousness as he tried to tackle his friend into the piny shrubs just off the sidewalk. In no time at all, both teens were laughing and wrestling like two hunchbacked bears, complete with overstuffed backpacks.

After the rolling and tumbling were over, Jake and Aaron got up and brushed themselves off as if it was perfectly normal to emerge from their neighbors' hedges covered in twigs and mulch. Not another intelligible word was shared the rest of the way to school. Between the laughter, shoves, and general trash talk, Jake and Aaron found a way to express the inexpressible—even with Wendy gone.

It seemed all too soon when they reached the central doors of the school. As they walked up the twelve steps to the main entrance, both Jake and Aaron wished that they had just kept walking past the building and down that same street forever.

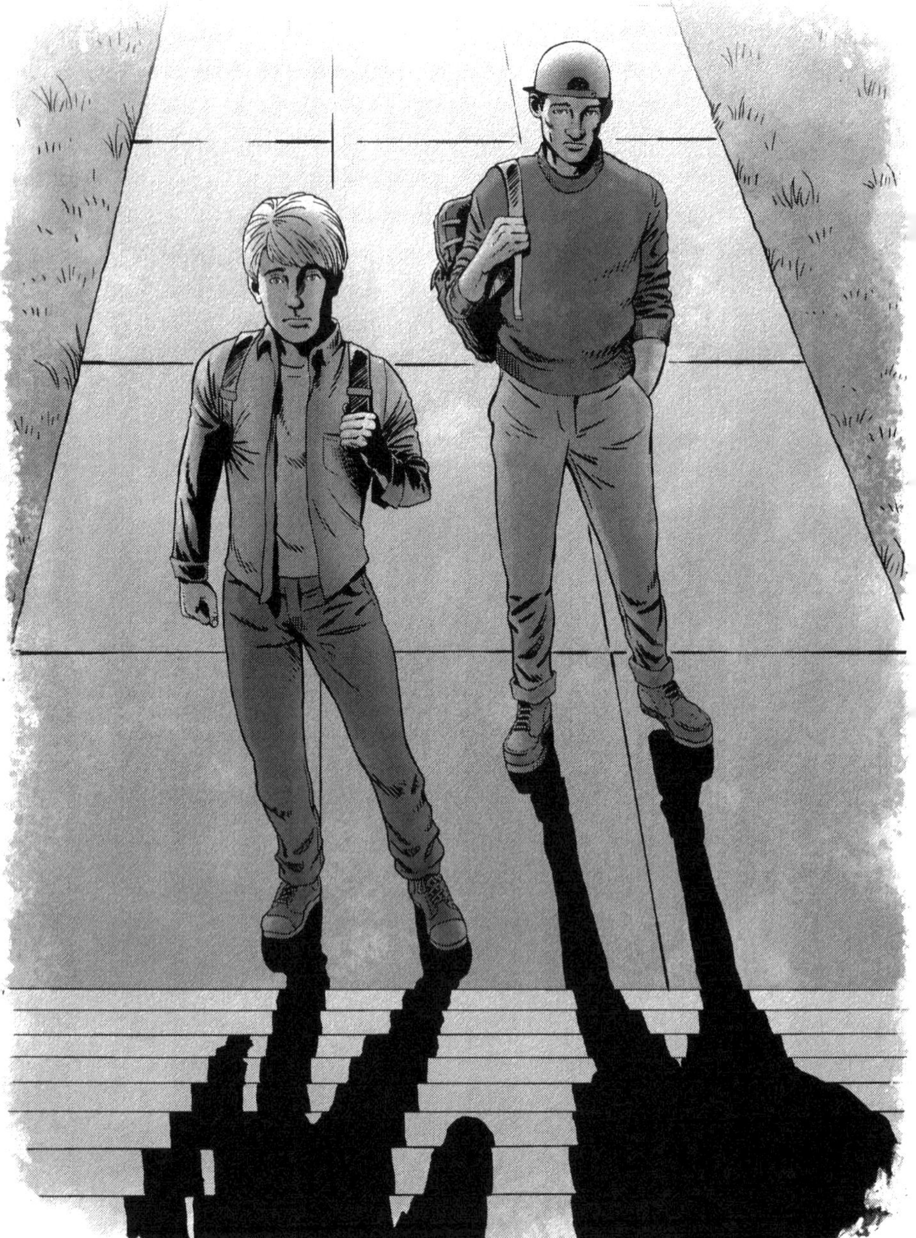

But they hadn't.

Instead, they stood on the threshold of a new day, knowing that everything in their lives was different. Aaron looked up from the porch steps at the massive windows that wrapped around the school in three rectangular rows. He had sat in those classrooms and looked out of those windows a thousand times. But he had never noticed them from the outside before. Standing on the outside looking in, they were like windows into the souls of many lives in his town. But the dirt and the glare clouded his vision from really seeing anything at all. He thought he knew what was inside that building like he thought he knew what was inside himself. How could everything be so familiar and yet so strange at the same time?

Jake grabbed the thick steel handle of the heavy metal door. The door swung open easily—much more easily than it was to walk through the doorway that framed it.

He held the door open wide and bowed deeply toward Aaron. Jake waved him forward with a dramatic, mocking gesture like a royal page preparing a grand entrance for his king. Aaron paused for a moment and looked directly into Jake's eyes. He knew what his friend was thinking. He understood the steps, the open door, and the voices that emanated from the old building, but little more than that.

The first-hour bell rang. Aaron smiled a little, shook his head, and walked past Jake, crossing the threshold into the school. His friend followed right behind him as the door shut with a resonating thud that echoed throughout the halls.

Neither of them noticed the shadows that hung silently in the air, staring in at them, just outside the first floor windows.

Explicit

(It has been unfolded)